D0041250

GALLANT

GALLANT

V. E. SCHWAB

GREENWILLOW BOOKS
An Imprint of HarperCollins*Publishers*

Gallant
Copyright © 2022 by Victoria Schwab
Interior illustrations copyright © 2022 by Manuel Šumberac

The text of this book is set in 11-point Baskerville No 2. BT.
Book design by Paul Zakris

Library of Congress Cataloging-in-Publication Data

Names: Schwab, V. E., author.
Title: Gallant / V. E. Schwab.
Description: First edition. | New York : Greenwillow Books, [2022] |
Audience: Ages 13 up | Audience: Grades 10-12 |
Summary: Olivia Prior has grown up at the grim Merilance School for Girls with no past except for her one treasure, her mother's journal, so when a letter arrives inviting her to come home to ruinous manor Gallant, she seizes the chance to find out about her family.
Identifiers: LCCN 2021044050 | ISBN 9780062835772 (hardback) |
ISBN 9780062835796 (ebook) | ISBN 9780063230255 (signed edition) | ISBN 9780063239180 (international pbk ed.) | ISBN 9780063253827 (OwlCrate ed.)
Subjects: CYAC: Orphans—Fiction. | Boarding schools—Fiction. |
Schools—Fiction. | Family secrets—Fiction. | LCGFT: Novels.
Classification: LCC PZ7.S39875 Gal 2022 | DDC [Fic]—dc23
LC record available at https://lccn.loc.gov/2021044050

22 23 24 25 26 PC/LSCH 10 9 8 7 6 5 4 3 2 1

First Edition

GREENWILLOW BOOKS

To those who go looking for doors,
are brave enough to open the ones they find,
and sometimes bold enough to make their own.

The master of the house stands at the garden wall.

It is a grim stretch of stone, an iron door locked and bolted at its center. There is a narrow gap between the door and the rock, and when the breeze is right, it carries the scent of summer, sweet as melon, and the distant warmth of sun.

There is no breeze tonight.

No moon, and yet he is bathed in moonlight. It catches the edges of his tattered coat. It shines on the bones where they show through his skin.

He trails his hand along the wall, searching for cracks. Stubborn strands of ivy follow in his wake, questing like fingers into every fissure, and nearby a bit of stone breaks free and tumbles to the ground, exposing a narrow slice of someone else's night. The culprit, a field mouse, scrambles through, and then down the wall, over the master's boot. He catches it in one hand, with all the grace of a snake.

He bends his head to the crack. Fastens his milk-white eyes on the other side. The other garden. The other house.

In his hand, the mouse squirms, and the master squeezes.

"Hush," he says, in a voice like empty rooms. He is listening to the other side, to the soft chirp of birdsong, the wind through lush leaves, the distant pleading of someone in their sleep.

The master smiles and picks up the bit of broken rock and nestles it back into the wall, where it waits, like a secret.

The mouse has stopped squirming in the cage of his grip.

When he opens his hand, there is nothing left but a streak of ash and rot and a few white teeth, little bigger than seeds.

He tips them out onto the wasted soil and wonders what will grow.

Part One

THE SCHOOL

Chapter One

Rain drums its fingers on the garden shed.

They call it a garden shed, but in truth there is no garden on the grounds of Merilance, and the shed is barely even that. It sags to one side, like a wilting plant, made of cheap metal and moldering wood. The floor is littered with abandoned tools and shards of broken pots and the stubs of stolen cigarettes, and Olivia Prior stands among them in the rusted dark, wishing she could scream.

Wishing she could turn the pain of the fresh red welt on her hand into noise, overturn the shed the way she did the pot in the kitchen when it burned her, strike the walls as she longed to strike Clara for leaving the stove on and having the nerve to snicker when Olivia gasped and let go. The white-hot pain, the red-hot anger, the cook's annoyance at the ruined mash, and Clara's pursed lips as she said, "It couldn't have hurt that much, she didn't make a sound."

Olivia would have wrapped her hands around the other girl's throat right there if her palm weren't singing, if the cook weren't there to haul her off, if the gesture would have gained her more than a moment's pleasure and a week's punishment. So she'd done the next best thing: stormed out of the stuffy tomb, the cook bellowing in her wake.

And now she's in the garden shed, wishing she could make as much noise as the rain on the low tin roof, take up one of the neglected spades and beat it against the thin metal walls, just to hear them ring. But someone else would hear, would come and find her, in this small and stolen place, and then she'd have nowhere to get away. Away from the girls. Away from the matrons. Away from the school.

She holds her breath and presses her burned hand against the cool metal shed, waiting for the ache in her skin to quiet.

The shed itself is not a secret.

It sits behind the school, across the gravel drive, at the back of the grounds. Over the years, a handful of girls have tried to claim it as their own, to smoke or drink or kiss, but they come once and never come back. It gives them the creeps, they say. Damp soil and spiderwebs, and something else, an eerie feeling that makes the hair stand up on their necks, though they don't know why.

But Olivia knows.

It is the dead thing in the corner.

Or what's left of it. Not a *ghost*, exactly, just a bit of tattered cloth, a handful of teeth, and a single, sleepy eye floating in the dark. It moves like a silverfish at the edge of Olivia's sight, darting away every time she looks. But if she stays very still and keeps her gaze ahead, it might grow a cheekbone, a throat. It might drift closer, might blink and smile and sigh against her, weightless as a shadow.

She has wondered, of course, who it was, back when it had bones and skin. The eye hovers, higher than her own, and once she caught the edge of a bonnet, the fraying hem of a skirt, and thought, perhaps, it was a matron. Not that it matters. Now, it is only a ghoul, lurking at her back.

Go away, she thinks, and perhaps it can hear her thoughts, because it flinches and draws back into the dark again, leaving her alone in the grim little shed.

Olivia leans back against the wall.

When she was younger, she liked to pretend that *this* was her house, not Merilance. That her mother and father had just stepped out and left her to clean up. They would be coming back, of course.

Once the house was ready.

Back then, she'd sweep away the dust and cobwebs, stack the pot shards and make order of the shelves. But no matter how tidy she tried to make the little shed, it was never clean enough to bring them back.

Home is a choice. Those four words sit alone on a page in her mother's book, surrounded by so much white space they feel like a riddle. In truth, everything her mother wrote feels like a riddle, waiting to be solved.

By now, the rain has slowed from pounding fists to the soft, infrequent tapping of bored fingers, and Olivia sighs and abandons the shed.

Outside, everything is gray.

The gray day is beginning to melt into a gray night, thin gray light lapping against the gray gravel path that surrounds the gray stone walls of Merilance School for Independent Girls.

The word "school" conjures images of neat wooden desks and scratching pencils. Of learning. They do learn, but it is a perfunctory education, spent on the practical. How to clean a fireplace. How to shape a loaf of bread. How to mend someone else's clothes. How to exist in a world that does not want you. How to be a ghost in someone else's home.

Merilance may call itself a school, but in truth, it is an asylum for the young and the feral and the fortuneless. The orphaned and unwanted. The dull gray building juts up like a tombstone, surrounded not by parks or rolling greens but the gaunt and sagging faces of the other structures at the city's edge, chimneys wheezing smoke. There are no walls around the place, no iron gates, only a vacant arch, as if to say, You're free to leave, if you have somewhere else to go. But if you go—and now and then, girls do—you will not be welcomed back. Once a year, sometimes more, a girl pounds at the door, desperate to get back in, and that is how the others learn that it's well and good to dream of happy lives and welcome homes, but even a grim tombstone of a place is better than the street.

And yet, some days Olivia is still tempted.

Some days, she eyes the arch, yawning like a mouth at the gravel's edge, and thinks, *what if*, thinks, *I could*, thinks, *one day I will*.

One night, she will break into the matrons' rooms and take whatever she can find and be gone. She will become a vagabond, a train robber, a cat burglar, or a con artist, like the men in the penny dreadfuls Charlotte always seems to have, tokens from a boy she meets at the edge of the gravel moat each week. Olivia plans a hundred different futures, but every night, she is still there, climbing into the narrow bed in the crowded room in the house that is not, and will never be, a home. And every morning she wakes up in the same place.

Olivia shuffles back across the yard, her shoes sliding over the gravel, with a steady *shh, shh, shh*. She keeps her eyes on the ground, searching for color. Now and then, after a good hard rain, a few green blades will force their way up between the pebbles, or a stubborn sheen of moss will latch onto a cobblestone, but these defiant colors never last. The only flowers she sees are in the head matron's office, and even those are fake and faded, silk petals long gone gray with dust.

And yet, as she rounds the school, heading for the side door she left ajar, Olivia sees a dash of yellow. A little weedy bloom, jutting up between the stones. She kneels, ignoring the way the pebbles bite into her knees, and brushes a careful thumb over the tiny flower. She's just about to pluck it when she hears the stomp of shoes on gravel, the familiar rustle and sigh of skirts that signal a matron.

They look the same, the matrons, in their once-white dresses with their once-white belts. But they're not. There's Matron Jessamine, with her tight little smile, as if she's sucking on a lemon, and Matron Beth, with her deep-set eyes and the bags beneath, and Matron Lara, with a voice as high and whining as a kettle.

And then, there's Matron Agatha.

"Olivia Prior!" she booms, in a breathless huff. "What are you doing?"

Olivia lifts her hands, even though she knows it's futile. Matron Sarah taught her how to sign, which was well and good until Matron Sarah left and none of the others bothered to learn.

Now it doesn't matter what Olivia says. No one knows how to listen.

Agatha stares at her as she shapes *planning my escape*, but she's only halfway through when the matron flaps her own hands, impatient.

"Where—is—your—chalkboard?" she asks, speaking loud and slow, as if Olivia is hard of hearing. She is not. As for the chalkboard, it's wedged behind a row of jam jars in the cellar, where it has been since it was first bestowed upon her, complete with a little rope to go around her neck.

"Well?" demands the matron.

Olivia shakes her head and picks the simplest sign for rain, repeating the gesture several times so the matron has a chance to see, but Agatha just *tsks* and grabs her wrist and hauls her back inside.

"You were supposed to be in the kitchen," says the matron, marching Olivia down the hall. "Now it's time for dinner, which you have not helped to make." *And yet, by some miracle,* thinks Olivia, judging by the scent wafting toward them, *it is ready.*

They reach the dining room, where girls' voices pile high, but the matron pushes her on, past the doors.

"Those who do not give, do not partake," she says, as if this is a Merilance motto and not something she's just thought up. She gives a curt little nod, pleased with herself, and Olivia pictures her stitching the words onto a pillow.

They reach the dormitory, where there are two dozen small shelves beside two dozen beds, thin and white as matchsticks, all of them empty.

"To bed," says the matron, though it isn't even dark. "Perhaps," she adds, "you can use this time to reflect on what it means to be a Merilance girl."

Olivia would rather eat glass, but she just nods and does her best to look contrite. She even curtsies once, bobbing her head low, but it is only so the matron cannot see the twist of her lips, the small, defiant smile. Let the old bat assume that she is sorry.

People assume a lot of things about Olivia.

Most of them are wrong.

The matron shuffles away, clearly not wanting to miss dinner, and Olivia steps into the dorm. She lingers at the foot of the first bed, listening to the rustle of receding skirts. As soon as Agatha has gone, she emerges again, slipping down the hall and around the corner to the matrons' quarters.

Each of the matrons has her own room. The doors are locked, but the locks are old and simple, the teeth on the keys little more than simple peaks.

Olivia draws a bit of sturdy wire from her pocket, remembering the shape of Agatha's key, the teeth a capital E. It takes a bit of fussing, but then the lock clicks, and the door swings open onto a neat little bedroom cluttered with pillows, little mantras embroidered across their fronts.

Here by the grace of God.

A place for all things, and all things in their place.

A house in order is a mind at peace.

Olivia's fingers trail over the words as she rounds the bed. A little mirror sits on the windowsill, and as she passes, she catches a glimpse of charcoal hair and a sallow cheek, and startles. But it is just her own reflection. Pale. Colorless. The ghost of Merilance. That's what the other girls call her. Yet there is a satisfying hitch in their voices, a hint of fear. Olivia looks at herself in the mirror. And smiles.

She kneels before the ash wood cabinet beside Agatha's bed. The matrons have their vices. Lara has cigarettes, and Jessamine has lemon drops, and Beth has penny dreadfuls. And Agatha?

Well. She has *several*. A bottle of brandy sloshes in the top drawer, and beneath that, Olivia finds a tin of cookies, iced with sugar, and a paper bag of clementines, bright as tiny sunsets. She takes three of the iced cookies and one piece of fruit, and retreats, silently, to the empty dorm to enjoy her dinner.

Chapter Two

Olivia lays the picnic out atop her narrow bed.

The cookies she eats fast, but the clementine she savors, peels it in a single curl, the sunny rind unraveling to reveal the happy segments. The whole room will smell like stolen citrus, but she doesn't care. It tastes like spring, like bare feet in grassy fields, like somewhere warm and green.

Her bed is at the far end of the room, so she can sit with her back to the wall as she eats, which is good, because it means she can keep her eye on the door. And the dead thing sitting on Clara's bed.

This ghoul is different, smaller than the other. It has knobby elbows and knees and an unblinking eye, one hand tugging on a tatty braid as it watches Olivia eat. There is something girlish in the way it moves. The way it pouts, and tips its head, and whispers in her ear when she's trying to sleep, soft and voiceless, the words nothing but air against her cheek.

Olivia scowls straight at it until it melts away.

That is the trick with the ghouls.

They want you to look, but they can't stand being seen.

At least, she thinks, they cannot touch her. Once, in a fit of frustration, she flung her hand out at a nearby ghoul, but her fingers went straight through. No eerie draft against her skin, not even the breath of something in the air. She felt better then, knowing it was not real enough, not *there* enough, to do more than smile or scowl or sulk.

Beyond the door, the sounds are changing.

Olivia listens to the shuffle and scrape of dinner ending down the hall, the rap of the head matron's cane as she stands to give her nightly lecture—on cleanliness, perhaps, or goodness, or modesty. Matron Agatha will be listening too, no doubt, ready to stitch the words onto a cushion.

From here, the speech is nothing but a rasp, a rustle—*Another mercy,* she thinks as she brushes the crumbs from the bed and hides the sunny ribbon of the orange peel under her pillow, where it will smell sweet. She reaches for the trinkets on her shelf.

Every bed has a shelf, though the contents change. Some girls have a doll, passed on as charity or sewn themselves. Some have a book they like to read, or a bit of embroidery on a hoop. Most of Olivia's shelf is taken up with sketchpads and a jar of pencils, worn short but sharp. (She is a gifted artist, and if the matrons of Merilance do not exactly nurture it, they don't neglect it either.) But tonight her fingers drift past the sketchpads to the green journal sitting at the end.

It was her mother's.

Her mother, who has always been a mystery, an empty space, an outline, the edges just firm enough to mark the absence. Olivia lifts the journal gently, running her hand over the cover, worn soft with age—the closest thing she has to a memory of life before Merilance. Olivia arrived at the grim stone tomb when she was not yet two, dirt-smudged in a dress trimmed with tiny wildflowers. She might have been out on the step for hours before they found her, they said, because she never cried. She doesn't remember that. Doesn't remember anything of the time before. She can't recall her mother's voice, and as for her father, she only knows she never met him. He was dead by the time she was born, that much she's gleaned from her mother's words.

It is a strange thing, the journal.

She has memorized every aspect, from the exact shade of green on the cover, to the elegant *G* scripted on its front—she has spent years guessing what it stands for, Georgina, Genevieve, Gabrielle—to the twin lines not pressed or scraped but *gouged* below it, perfect parallel grooves that run from one edge to the other. From the strange ink blooms that take up entire pages to the entries in her mother's hand, some long and others only a handful of words, some lucid, and others cracked and broken, all of them addressed to "you."

When Olivia was small, she thought that *she* was the "you," that her mother was speaking to her across time, those three letters a hand, reaching through paper.

If you read this, I am safe.

I dreamed of you last night.

Do you remember when . . .

But eventually, she came to understand the "you" was someone else: her father.

Though he never answers, her mother writes on as if he has, entry after entry full of strange, veiled terms of their courtship, of birds in cages, of starless skies, writing of his kindness and her love and fear, and then, at last, of Olivia. *Our daughter.*

But there her mother begins to unravel. She begins to write of shadows crawling like fingers through the dark, and voices carried on the wind, calling her home. Soon her graceful script begins to tip, before tumbling over the cliff into madness.

That cliff? The night her father died.

He was ill. Her mother spoke of it, the way he seemed to wane as her belly waxed, some wasting sickness that stole him weeks before Olivia was born. And when he died, her mother fell. She broke. Her lovely words went jagged, the writing came apart.

I am sorry I wanted to be free sorry I opened the door sorry you're not here and they are watching he is watching he wants you back but you are gone he wants me but I won't go he wants her but she is all I have of you and me she is all she is all I want to go home

Olivia doesn't like to linger on these pages, in part because they are the ramblings of a woman gone mad. And in part because she's forced to wonder if that madness is the kind that lingers in the blood. If it sleeps inside her, too, waiting to be woken.

The writing eventually ends, replaced by nothing but a blank expanse, until, near the back, a final entry. A letter, addressed not to a father, living or dead, but to *her*.

Olivia Olivia Olivia, her mother writes, the name unravelling across the page, and her gaze drifts over the ink-spotted paper, fingers tracing the tangled words, the lines drawn through abandoned text as her mother fought to find her way through the thicket of her thoughts.

Something flickers at the edge of Olivia's sight. The ghoul, nearer now, peers sheepishly over the mound of Clara's pillow. It tilts its head, as if listening, and Olivia does the same. She can hear them coming. She shuts the journal.

Seconds later, the doors swing open and the girls pour in.

They chirp and chime as they spill across the room. The younger ones glance her way and whisper, but as soon as she looks back, they skitter past, like insects, to the safety of their sheets. The older ones do not look at all. They pretend she is not there, but she knows the truth: They are afraid. She has made sure of it.

Olivia was ten when she showed her teeth.

Ten, and walking down the hall, only to hear her mother's words in someone else's mouth.

"These dreams will be the death of me," it said. *"When I am dreaming, I know that I must wake. But when I wake, all I think about is dreaming."*

She reached the dorms to find silver-blonde Anabelle sitting primly on her bed, reading the entry to a handful of snickering girls.

"In my dreams, I am always losing you. In my waking, you are already lost."

The words sounded wrong in Anabelle's high lilt, her mother's madness on full display. Olivia marched over and tried to take the journal back, but Anabelle darted out of reach, flashing a wicked grin.

"If you want it," she said, holding the journal aloft, "all you have to do is ask."

Olivia's throat tightened. Her mouth opened, but nothing came out, just a rush of air, an angry breath.

Anabelle snickered at her silence. And Olivia lunged. Her fingers skimmed the journal, before two more girls pulled her back.

"Ah, ah, ah," teased Anabelle, wagging a finger. "You have to *ask*." She sidled closer. "You don't even have to shout." She leaned in, as if Olivia could simply whisper, shape the word *please* and set it free. Her teeth clicked together.

"What's wrong with her?" sneered Lucy, scrunching up her nose.

Wrong.

Olivia scowled at the word. As if she hadn't stolen into the infirmary the year before, hadn't scoured the anatomy book, hadn't found the drawings of the human mouth and throat and copied every single one, hadn't sat up in bed that night, feeling along the lines of her own neck, trying to trace the source of her silence, trying to find exactly what was missing.

"Go on," goaded Anabelle, holding the journal high. And when Olivia still said nothing, the girl flicked open the book that was not hers, exposing the words that were not hers, touching the paper that was not hers, and began to tear the pages out.

That sound, the ripping of paper from seam, was the loudest in the world, and Olivia tore free of the other girls' hands and fell on Anabelle, fingers wrapped around her throat. Anabelle yelped, and Olivia squeezed until the girl could not speak, could not breathe, and then the matrons were there, pulling them apart.

Anabelle sobbed, and Olivia scowled, and both girls were sent to bed without supper.

"It was just a bit of fun." The other girl sulked, collapsing onto her bed as Olivia silently, painstakingly, tucked the torn pages back into her mother's journal, holding close the memory of Anabelle's throat beneath her hands. Thanks to the anatomy book, she'd known exactly where to squeeze.

Now she runs her finger down the journal's edge, where the torn pages stick out farther than the rest. Her dark eyes flick up as she watches the girls file in.

There is a moat around Olivia's bed. That is what it feels like. A small, invisible stream that no one will cross, rendering her cot a castle. A fortress.

The younger girls think she is cursed.

The older ones think she is feral.

Olivia doesn't care, so long as they leave her alone.

Anabelle is the last one in.

Her pale eyes dart to Olivia's corner, one hand going to her silver-blonde braid. Olivia feels a smile rise to her lips.

That night, after the torn-out pages were safely back inside their book, after the lights were out and the girls of Merilance were all asleep, Olivia got up. She crept into the kitchen, and took an empty mason jar, and went down into the cellar, the kind of place that is somehow always dry and damp at once. It took an hour, maybe two, but she managed to fill the jar with beetles, and spiders, and half a dozen silverfish. She added a handful of ash from the head matron's hearth, so the little bugs would leave their mark, and then she crept back into the dormitory and opened the jar over Anabelle's head.

The other girl woke screaming.

Olivia watched from her bed as Anabelle pawed at the sheets and tumbled out onto the floor. Around the room, the girls all shrieked, and the matrons came in time to see a silverfish wriggle out of Anabelle's braid. Nearby, the ghoul watched, shoulders bobbing in a silent chuckle, and as Anabelle was led sobbing from the room, the ghoul held up a bony finger to its half-formed lips, as if vowing to keep the secret. But Olivia didn't want it to be a secret. She wanted Anabelle to know exactly who'd done it. She wanted her to know who made her scream.

By breakfast, Anabelle's hair had been lopped short. She

looked straight at Olivia, and Olivia stared back.

Go on, she thought, holding the other girl's gaze. *Say something.*

Anabelle didn't.

But she never touched the journal again.

It's been years now, and Anabelle's silver-blonde hair has long grown back, but she still touches the braid every time she sees Olivia, the way the girls are told to cross themselves or kneel at service.

Every time, Olivia smiles.

"Into bed," says a matron—it doesn't matter which. And soon the lights go out, and the room is still. Olivia climbs beneath the scratchy blanket and curls her spine into the wall and hugs the journal to her chest and closes her eyes against the ghoul and the girls and the world of Merilance.

Olivia Olivia Olivia

I have been whispering the name into your hair
~~so you will remember~~ *will you remember?*
~~I don't know I can't~~ *They say there is love in*
letting go but I feel only loss. My heart is ash and
~~did you know ash holds its shape until you touch it~~
I do not want to leave you but I no longer trust myself
~~there is no time there is no time there is no time to~~
I'm so sorry I don't know what else to do
Olivia, Olivia, Olivia, Remember this—
the shadows ~~cannot touch~~ *are not real*
the dreams ~~are only dreams~~ *can never hurt you*
and you will be safe as long as you stay away
from Gallant

Chapter Three

Olivia has been buried alive.

At least, that is how it feels. The kitchen is such a stuffy place, in the bowels of the building, the air clogged with pot steam and the walls made of stone, and whenever Olivia is forced to work in here, she feels as if she's been entombed. She wouldn't mind it so much, if she were alone.

There are no ghouls down in the kitchen, but there are always girls. They chitter and chat, filling the room with noise, just because they can. One is telling a story about a prince and a palace. One is moaning about cramps, and the other sits on the counter, swinging her legs and doing absolutely nothing.

Olivia tries to ignore them, focusing instead on her bowl of potatoes, the paring knife glinting dully in her palm. She studies her hands as she works. They are thin, unlovely but strong. Hands that can speak, though few at the school bother to listen, hands that can write and draw and stitch a perfect line. Hands that can part skin from flesh without slipping.

There *is* a small scar, between her finger and thumb, but that was a long time ago, and it was her own doing. She had heard the other girls holler when they hurt themselves. A sharp cry, a long wail. Hell, when Lucy tried to jump between the cots one day and missed and broke her foot, she bellowed. And Olivia had wondered, almost absently one day, if her voice lay on the other side of some threshold, if it could be summoned forth with pain.

The knife was sharp. The cut was deep. Blood welled and spilled onto the counter, and heat screamed up her arm and through her lungs, but only a short, sharp gasp escaped her throat, more emptiness than sound.

When Clara saw the blood, she yelped, a high disgusted noise, and Amelia called for the matrons, who assumed it was an accident, of course. Clumsy thing, they tutted and tsked, while the other girls whispered. Everyone, it seemed, so full of noise. Except Olivia.

She, who *wanted* to scream, not in pain but sheer exasperated fury that there was so much noise inside her, and she could not let it out. She'd kicked over a pile of pots instead, just to hear them clang.

Across the kitchen, the girls have turned to talk of love.

They whisper as if it's a secret or a stolen sweet, palmed and kept inside their cheeks. As if love is all they need. As if they have been placed under a curse and only love will set them free. She does not see the point in that: love did not save her father from illness and death. It did not save her mother from madness and loss.

The girls say *love*, but what they really mean is *want*. To be wanted, beyond the walls of this house. They are waiting to be rescued by one of the boys who linger at the edge of the gravel moat, trying to lure them across.

Olivia rolls her eyes at the mention of favors and promises and futures.

"What would *you* know?" sneers Rebecca, catching the look. She is a reedy girl with eyes too small and too close. More than once, Olivia has drawn her as a weasel. "Who would want *you?*"

Little does she know, there was a boy that spring. He caught her coming from the shed. Their eyes met, and he smiled.

"Come talk to me," he said, and Olivia frowned and withdrew into the house. But the next day, he was there again, a yellow daisy in one hand. "For you," he said, and she wanted the flower more than his attention, but still she drifted across the moat. Up close, his hair caught like copper in the sun. Up close, he smelled of soot. Up close, she noticed his lashes, and his lips, with the distance of an artist studying her subject.

When he kissed her, she waited to feel whatever her mother had felt for her father, the day they met, the spark that lit the fire that burned their whole world down. But she only felt his hand on her waist. His mouth on her mouth. A hollow sadness.

"Don't you want it?" he'd asked when his hand grazed her ribs.

She wanted to want it, to feel what the other girls felt.

But she didn't. And yet, Olivia is full of *want*. She wants a bed that does not creak. A room without Anabelles or matrons or ghouls. A window and a grassy view and air that does not taste of soot and a father who does not die and a mother who does not leave and a future beyond the walls of Merilance.

She wants all those things, and she has been here long enough to know that it does not matter what *you* want—the only way out is to be wanted by someone else.

She knows, and still, she pushed him away.

And the next time she saw the boy, at the edge of the yard, he was leaning toward another girl, a pretty little wisp named Mary, who giggled and whispered in his ear. Olivia waited for the flush of envy, but all she felt was cool relief.

She finishes skinning a potato and studies the little paring knife. Balances it on the back of her hand before flicking it gingerly into the air and catching the grip. She smiles, then, a small private thing.

"Freak," mutters Rebecca. Olivia looks up, holds her eye, and wags the knife like a finger. Rebecca scowls and turns her attention to the other girls, as if Olivia is a ghoul, something to be ignored.

They move on from boys, at least. Now they are talking about dreams.

"I was at the seaside."

"You've never been to the sea."

"So what?"

Olivia takes up another potato, slides the knife under the

starchy skin. She is almost done, but she slows her work, listening to them prattle.

"So how do you know it was the seaside and not a lake?"

"There were seagulls. And rocks. And besides, you don't need to know about a place to dream of it."

"Of course you do . . ."

Olivia quarters the spud and drops it in the pot.

They talk of dreams as if they're solid things, the kind you might mistake for real. They wake with whole stories impressed upon their minds, images committed to memory.

Her mother spoke of dreams as well, but hers were crueler things, filled with dead lovers and clawing shadows, sharp enough that she felt the need to warn her daughter they were not real.

But her mother's warning is wasted.

Olivia has never had a dream.

She *imagines* things, of course, conjures other lives, pretends she is someone else—a girl with a large family and a grand house and a garden bathed in sun, fanciful things like that—but not once, in fourteen years, has she been visited by dreams. Sleep, when it comes, is a dark tunnel, a shroud of black. Sometimes, right after she wakes, there is a kind of filament, like spider silk, clinging to her skin. That strange sense of something just out of reach, an image bobbing on the surface before rippling away. But then it's gone.

"Olivia."

Her name cuts through the air. She flinches, fingers tensing on the knife, but it is only the thin-faced matron, Jessamine, waiting at the door, lips pursed as if she's got a lemon on her tongue. She crooks her finger, and Olivia abandons her station.

Heads swivel. Eyes follow her out.

"What has she done now?" they whisper, and honestly, she doesn't know. It could have been the lockpicks she fashioned, or the sweets she stole from Matron Agatha's drawer, or the chalkboard buried in the cellar.

She shivers a little as they climb the stairs, trading the stuffy kitchen for the chilly halls beyond. Her heart sinks at the sight of the head matron's door. Never a good sign, to be summoned here.

Jessamine knocks, and a voice answers from the other side.

"Come in."

Olivia clenches her jaw, teeth clicking softly together as she steps inside.

It is a narrow room. The walls are lined with books, which would be welcoming if they were stories of magic or pirates or thieves. Instead, thick spines bear titles like *The Lady's Book of Etiquette* and *Pilgrim's Progress,* and a full shelf of encyclopedias that as far she knows have only been used to enforce good posture.

"Miss Prior," says the bony figure at the dark wood desk.

The head matron of Merilance is old. She has always been old. Aside from the addition of a few new wrinkles in an already-lined face, she has not changed in all the time Olivia has lived here. Her shoulders do not hunch, her pale eyes never blink, and her voice, when she speaks, is as thin and efficient as a switch.

"Sit."

There are two chairs in the room. A thin wooden one against the wall, and a faded green one before the desk.

The one against the wall is already taken. A thin little ghoul sits, bent forward, legs swinging back and forth, too short to touch the floor. Olivia stares at the half-formed girl, wondering who would choose to haunt this room of all the ones in Merilance.

The head matron clears her throat. The sound is a bony hand, pinching Olivia's chin.

The ghoul dissolves back into the wooden boards, and Olivia forces herself forward and takes a seat in the faded green chair, sending up a plume of dust. She stares blandly at the old woman, hoping the expression reads as dull, but unfortunately, the head matron of Merilance has never been polite enough to underestimate Olivia. To take her silence for stupidity, or even disinterest. Laid before the old woman's blue-eyed gaze she feels unmoored, exposed.

"You have been with us for quite some time," says the head matron, as if Olivia doesn't know. As if she's lost track of the years, the way a prisoner might within a cell. "We have cared for you since you were a child. Nurtured you as you grew into a young woman."

Nurtured. Grew. As if she were a houseplant. She studies the dusty silk roses that sit on the old woman's desk, the color leeched by window light, tries to remember a time when they were anything but gray. And then the head matron does a terrible thing.

She *smiles*.

There was a cat one year at Merilance. A feral little beast that hung around the garden shed, catching mice. It would stretch out atop the tin roof, tail flicking and belly full, its mouth curled in a smug little grin. The head matron wears the same expression.

"And now, your time here has come to an end."

Olivia's whole body tenses. She knows what happens to the girls when they leave Merilance, sent to wither in a workhouse or gifted like a prize pig to a middle-aged man or buried in the bowels of someone else's house.

"There are not many prospects, you know, for a girl in your . . . condition."

Olivia peels the skin from the words. What the head matron means is that there are not many futures for a high-tempered orphan who cannot speak. She'd make a fine wife, she's been told, save for her temper. She'd make a fine maid, save for the fact so many take her silence as a sign of some greater ill, or at the least, find it unnerving. What does that leave? Nothing good. Her mind races through the halls, planning an escape; there is still time to raid the matrons' cupboards, still time to flee into the city, to find another way—but the head matron taps her bony fingers on the desk, calling her back.

"Fortunately," she says, sliding open a drawer, "the matter seems to have been sorted for us."

With that, she produces an envelope. And even before she hands it over, Olivia can see that it's addressed to *her*. Her name curls across the envelope in peculiar cursive, the letters falling slantwise like rain.

Olivia Prior

The top of the envelope has been torn open, the contents removed and then returned, and she feels a brief, indignant flare at the invasion. But annoyance quickly gives way to curiosity as the head matron passes her the envelope, and she withdraws the letter, written in the same strange hand.

"My dearest niece," it begins.

I confess, I do not know exactly where you are.

I have sent these letters to every corner of the country. May this be the one that finds you.

Here is what I know. When you were born, your mother was not well. She took you and fled from us, pursued by delusions of danger. I fear that she is dead and can only hope that you still live. You must think yourself abandoned, but it is not so. It has never been so.

You are wanted. You are needed. You belong with us.
Come home, dear niece.
We cannot wait to welcome you.

Your uncle,
Arthur Prior

Olivia reads the letter again, and again, her mind spinning.

Niece. Uncle. Home. She does not realize how hard she's gripping the letter until it crumples.

"Fate has smiled on you, Miss Prior," says the head matron, but Olivia cannot take her eyes from the paper. She turns the envelope over, and there on the back is an address. The words and letters jumble, meaningless, in her mind, aside from the word at the top.

Gallant.

Olivia's ribs seem to tighten around her heart.

She traces her thumb over the word, the same one that ended her mother's journal. It never made sense. Once, long ago, she'd looked it up in one of the matron's heavy dictionaries, learned that it meant brave, especially in trying times. Courage under duress. But for her mother—for Olivia—it is not a description. It is a *place*. A *home*. The word washes over her like a high tide, knocking her off balance. She feels a little dizzy, a little ill.

Come home, the letter says.

Stay away, her mother warned.

But here her uncle says, *Your mother was not well.* That much has always been clear from the journal, but they were her mother's final words, surely she had a reason for—

The head matron clears her throat. "I suggest you go collect your things," she says, hand flicking to the door. "It is a long drive, and the car will be here soon."

I am so happy. I am so scared.
The two, it turns out, can walk together, hand in hand.

Chapter Four

The ghoul sits cross-legged on a nearby bed, watching as Olivia packs.

One eye floats above a narrow chin, the features broken up by sunlight. It looks almost sad to see her go.

The matrons have given her a slim suitcase, just large enough to fit her two gray dresses, her sketchpads, her mother's journal. She tucks her uncle's letter in the back, his invitation side by side with her mother's warning.

You will be safe, as long as you stay away.

We cannot wait to welcome you.

One mad, the other absent, and she doesn't know which to believe, but in the end it doesn't matter. The letter might as well be a summons. And perhaps she should be afraid of the unknown, but curiosity beats a drum inside her chest. She is leaving. She has somewhere to go.

A home.

Home is a choice, her mother wrote, and even though she has not chosen Gallant, perhaps she will. After all, you can choose a thing after it's chosen you. And even if it turns out not to be a home, it is at least a house with family waiting in it.

A black car idles in the gravel moat. She has seen these cars come to Merilance, summoned by the head matron when it is time for a girl to go. A parting gift, a one-way ride. The door hangs open like a mouth, waiting to swallow her up, and fear prickles beneath her skin, even as she tells herself, *Anywhere is better than here.*

The matrons stand on the steps like sentinels. The other girls do not come to see her off, but the doors are open, and she catches the silver whip of Anabelle's braid glinting in the hall.

Good riddance, she thinks, climbing into the belly of the beast. The engine turns, and the tires churn across the gravel moat. They pull through the arch and out onto the street, and Olivia watches through the back window as the garden shed vanishes and Merilance falls away. One moment, it is shrinking. The next, it is gone, swallowed up by the surrounding buildings and the plumes of coal smoke.

Something wriggles inside her then, half terror and half thrill. Like when you take the stairs too fast and almost slip. The moment when you catch yourself and look down at what could have happened, some disaster narrowly escaped.

The car rumbles beneath her, the only sound as the city thins, the buildings sinking from three stories to two, two to one, before growing gaps, like bad teeth. And then something marvelous happens. They reach the *end* of all those buildings, all that smoke and soot and steam. The last houses give way to rolling hills, and the world transforms from gray to green.

Olivia opens the suitcase and plucks her uncle's letter from the journal.

My dearest niece, he wrote, and she holds on to the promise in those words.

She reads the letter again, soaking in the ink, scouring the words and the space between for answers and finding none. Something wafts off the paper, like a draft. She brings the letter to her nose. It is summer, and yet, the parchment smells of autumn, brittle and dry, that narrow season when nature withers and dies, when the windows are shuttered and the furnaces belch smoke and winter waits like a promise, just out of sight.

Outside, the sun breaks through, and she looks up to find fields unraveling to either side, heather, wheat, and tallgrass blowing softly in the breeze. She wants to climb out, to abandon the car, sprawl among the waving blades and spread her arms the way the girls did when it snowed last year, even though it was only an inch of white and they could feel the gravel every time they moved.

But she does not climb out, and the car drives on through the countryside. She doesn't know how far they're going. No one told her, not the head matron before she left, not the driver who sits up front, fingers tapping on the wheel.

She slips the letter in her pocket, holds it there like a token, a talisman, a key. Then she turns her attention to the journal, lying open in her lap. The window is cracked, and the pages turn in the breeze, airy fingers flipping past scribbled entries inter-rupted here and there by stretches of darkness. Pools of black that look like spills until you squint and realize there are shapes inside the shadows.

Not accidents at all but *drawings*.

So unlike the careful sketches in Olivia's own pads, these are wild, abstract blooms of ink that swallow up entire pages, bleed-ing through parchment. And even though they sprawl across the pages of her mother's book, they feel as though they don't belong.

They are strange, even beautiful, organic things that shift and curl across the page, slowly resolving into shapes. Here is a hand. Here is a hall. Here is a man, the shadows twisting at his feet. Here is a flower. Here is a skull. Here is a door flung open onto—what? Or who? Or where?

As beautiful as they are, Olivia does not like to look at the pictures.

They unsettle her, skittering across her sight like silverfish on the cellar floor. They make her eyes blur and her head ache, the way they almost come together, only to fall apart again, like ghouls, under her scrutiny.

The breeze picks up, tugging at the loose pages, and she closes the journal, forcing her gaze to the sunny fields rolling past beyond the window.

"Not a chatty thing, are you?" says the driver. He has a coarse accent, like his mouth is full of pebbles that he's trying not to swallow.

Gallant

Olivia shakes her head, but it's as if a seal has broken now, and the driver keeps talking in an absent, winding way, about children and goats and the weather. People tend to talk to Olivia, or rather, *at* her, some uneasy with the silence, others treating it as an invitation. She doesn't mind this time, her own attention captured by the vivid world outside, the fields so many different shades of green.

"Never been this far north," he muses, glancing over his shoulder. "Have you?"

Olivia shakes her head again, though in truth, she doesn't know. There was a time before Merilance, after all, but it holds no shape, nothing but a stretch of mottled black. And yet, the longer they drive, the more she feels that darkness flicker, giving way, not to memories, but simply the space where they would be.

Perhaps it is only her mind playing tricks.

Perhaps it is the word—*home*—or the knowledge that some-one is waiting for her there, the idea that she is wanted.

It is after lunch when they enter a charming little town, and her heart ticks up as the car slows, hopeful that this is it, this is Gallant, but the driver only wants to stretch and get a snack. He climbs out, groaning as his bones pop and crack. Olivia follows, startled by the warmth in the air, the clouds shot through with sun.

He buys a pair of meat pies from a shop and hands one out to her. She has no money, but her stomach growls, loud enough for him to hear, and he presses the hot crust into her palm. She signs a *thank you*, but he either doesn't see or doesn't understand.

Olivia looks around, wondering how much farther they're going, and the question must be written on her face because he says, "A while yet." He takes a bite of meat pie and nods at the distant hills, which look taller and more wild than the land they've driven through. "Imagine we'll be there before dark."

They finish eating, wiping their greasy hands on the wax paper, and the engine starts again. Olivia settles back in the seat, warm and full, and soon the world is nothing but the rumbling car and the tires on the road and the occasional musings of the driver.

She doesn't mean to fall asleep, but when she wakes, the light is thin, the shadows long, the sky above streaked pink and gold with dusk. Even the ground has changed beneath the car, from a proper road to a rough dirt lane. The hills have been replaced by stony mountains, distant craggy shapes that rise to either side like waves, and the grim walls of Merilance with its soot-stained sky feel worlds away.

"Not far now," says the driver as they follow the winding road, through copses of ancient trees and over narrow bridges and around a rocky bend. It comes out of nowhere, the gate.

Two stone pillars with a word arched in iron overhead.

GALLANT

Her heart begins to race as the car trundles forward, down the lane. A shape rises in the distance, and the driver whistles under his breath.

"Lucky thing, aren't you?" he says, because Gallant is not just a house. It is an *estate,* a mansion twice the size of Merilance and so many times grander. It has a roof that peaks like egg whites, carved windows and walls of pale stone that catch the sunset the way a canvas catches paint. Wings unfold on either side, and grand old trees stand at its edges, their limbs flung wide, and between their trunks, she can even see a garden. Hedges, roses, wild blooms peering out from behind the house.

Olivia's mouth hangs open. It is a dream, the closest she has ever come, and she's afraid to wake. She drinks it all in like a girl dying of thirst, in desperate gulps, has to remind herself to stop, and breathe, and sip, remind herself that there will be time. That she is not a passing stranger on the grounds.

The driver guides the car around a stately fountain, a stone figure standing at its center. A woman, dress rippling behind her as if caught in a gust of wind. She stands with her back to the massive house, her head held high, and one hand raised, palm out, as if reaching, and as the car rounds the fountain, Olivia half expects the woman to turn her head and watch them pass, but of course, she doesn't. Her stone eyes stay on the lane and the arch and the failing light.

"Here we are, then," says the driver, easing the car to a stop. The engine quiets, and he climbs out, fetching her slim suitcase and setting it on the stairs. Olivia steps down, her legs stiff from so many hours folded into the back seat. He gives a shallow bow and a soft "Welcome home" and climbs back behind the wheel. The engine rumbles to life.

And then he's gone, and Olivia is alone.

She turns in a slow circle, gravel crunching beneath her shoes. The same pale gravel that lined the moat at Merilance, that whispered *shh, shh, shh* with every skating step, and for a second, her world lurches, and she looks up, expecting to find the tombstone face of the school, the garden shed, a matron waiting, arms crossed, to drag her in again.

But there is no Merilance, no matron, only Gallant.

Olivia approaches the fountain, fingers itching to draw the woman there. But up close, the pool of water at her feet is still, stagnant, its edges green. Up close, there's something ominous in the tilt of the woman's chin, her raised hand less a welcome than a warning. A command. Stop.

She shivers. It's getting dark so quickly, dusk plunging into night, and a cool breeze has blown through, stealing the last of the summer warmth. She cranes her neck, studying the house. The shutters are all closed, but the edges are traced with light.

Olivia heads toward the house, takes up her suitcase, and climbs the four stone steps that lead from the drive to the front doors, solid wood marked by a single iron circle, cold beneath her fingers.

Olivia holds her breath and knocks.

And waits.

But no one comes.

She knocks again. And again. And somewhere between the fourth knock and the fifth, the fear she kept at bay, first in the head matron's office, and then in the car as it carried her from Merilance, the fear of the unknown, of a dream dissolving back into a grim gray truth, finally catches up. It wraps its arms around her, it slides under her skin, it winds around her ribs.

What if no one is home?

What if she has come all this way and—

But then the bolt draws back, and the door swings open. Not all the way, just enough for a woman to look out. She is stout, with rough-hewn edges and wild brown curls, threaded with silver. She has the kind of face Olivia has always loved to draw— every emotion played out on skin, open, expressive. And right now, every line and crease folds into a frown.

"What in God's name . . ." She trails off at the sight of Olivia, then looks past her to the empty drive, and back again. "Who are you?"

Olivia's heart sinks, just a little. But of course they would not know her, not by sight. The woman studies her as if she is a stray cat that's wandered by accident onto their step, and Olivia realizes she is waiting for her to speak. To explain herself. She reaches for the letter in her pocket as a man's voice pours down the hall.

"Hannah, who is it?" he calls, and Olivia looks past the

woman, hoping to see her uncle. But when the door opens wider, she knows at a glance that it's not him. This man's skin is several shades darker than her own, his face too thin, his bearing winnowed with age.

"I don't know, Edgar," says the woman—Hannah. "It appears to be a girl."

"How odd . . ."

The door swings wider, and as the light spills over Olivia's face, the woman's eyes go wide.

"No . . ." she says softly, an answer to a question she didn't voice. Then, "How did you get here?"

Olivia offers up her uncle's letter. The woman's eyes dart over the envelope, then the contents within. And even in the thin hall light, she can see the last of the color go out of the woman's face. "I don't understand." She turns the paper over, searching for more.

"What is it?" presses Edgar, but Hannah only shakes her head, her gaze returning to Olivia, and though Olivia has always been good at reading faces, she cannot make sense of what she sees. Confusion. Concern. And something else.

The woman opens her mouth, a question forming on her lips, but then her eyes narrow, not on Olivia, but the yard behind her.

"You best come in," she says. "Out of the dark."

Olivia looks back over her shoulder. The sunset has bled away, the night deepening around them. She is not afraid of the dark—has never been, but the man and woman seem unnerved by it. Hannah opens the door wide, revealing a well-lit foyer, a massive staircase, a maze of a house.

"Hurry up," she says.

It is hardly the welcome she expected, but Olivia gathers her suitcase and steps inside, and the door swings shut behind her, walling off the night.

The master of the house is not alone.

He has three shadows, one short, one thin, one broad, and they watch as he rises from his chair, falling silently behind as shadows do.

There is a space between the second and the third, and a keen observer might guess that once, perhaps, there had been four. Perhaps, but now there are only three, and they follow their master as he makes his way through the house that is and is not empty.

There are dead things watching from the corners. Things that once were human. They bow their ghoulish heads and shrink back as the master and his shadows pass, making themselves small in the hollows of the house. Now and then, one glances up and glares, eyes sharp. Now and then, one remembers how they came to be in there in the dark.

The master drags his nails against the wall and hums, the sound carrying like a draft. There are other noises—the wind outside whispers through the tattered curtains, and a piece of plaster cracks and crumbles free, and the whole place seems to groan and tilt and sink—but the ghouls are silent, and the shadows cannot speak, so his is the only voice that carries through the house.

Part Two

THE HOUSE

Chapter Five

Olivia has never been in such a house.

The foyer arches like the bones of some great beast, and lamps fill the space with soft yellow light, and she looks around, marveling at everything she sees: the grand staircase, the high ceilings and ornate floors. Her eyes skip from painting to pattern, wallpaper to rug to glass to door as Hannah ushers her out of the foyer and down the hall into a sitting room, two chairs and a sofa arranged before the fire. Olivia scans the room, searching the edges of her sight, but there are no teeth, no eyes, no signs of ghouls. She looks to Hannah and Edgar, expecting one of them to fetch her uncle, but they just stand in the doorway, trading quick, hushed words as if she cannot hear.

"Just read it," says Hannah, pressing the letter into his hands.

"It makes no sense."

"Did Arthur even know . . ."

"He would have said something. . . ."

Edgar frowns. "She looks just like—"

"Grace."

There is an ache in the way Hannah says the name, and in that moment she knows—she *knows*—that the *G* on the front of her mother's journal, the one worn to nothing by her fingertips, stood not for Georgina, or Genevieve, or Gabrielle, but *Grace*. Relief pours through her. They knew her mother. Perhaps they know what happened to her.

"Olivia," says Edgar, as if testing out the name. "Where did you come from?"

She gestures at the envelope, the address scrawled across its front. *Merilance School for Independent Girls.*

Hannah frowns, not at the letter but at her. "Have you lost your voice?"

Anger spikes through her. *No*, she signs, the gestures sharp, deliberate. *I didn't lose it.*

The retort is only for herself, of course. She knows they will not understand.

Or so she thinks, until Edgar answers. "I'm sorry." He signs as he says it, and she spins toward him, spirits lifting. It has been so long since she could speak with someone, and her fingers are already flying through the air.

But he holds up his hands. "Slow down," he pleads, signing the words. "I'm very rusty."

She nods and tries again, shaping the first question carefully. *Where is my uncle?*

Edgar translates, and Hannah's brow furrows. "When did you receive this letter?"

Olivia signs. *Today.*

Edgar shakes his head. "That's not possible," he says. "Arthur has been—"

Just then, footsteps sound in the hall.

"Hannah?" calls a voice, and moments later a boy strides in, studying a pair of gardening gloves. He is older than Olivia by several years, nearly a man, tall and sapling thin, with tawny hair. "I think the thorns are getting sharper," he says. "There's another tear here, near the thumb and—"

He looks up at last and sees her standing by the fire.

"Who are you?" he demands, the softness melting from his voice.

"Matthew," says Hannah. "This is Olivia." A moment's pause, and then, "Your cousin."

Uncle. Niece. And now, a cousin. All her life, Olivia has dreamed of family, of waking up one day and learning she was not alone. *Matthew* does not take the news so well. He recoils from the words, as if struck. "That's ridiculous. There are no more Priors."

"Apparently there are," says Edgar gently, as if her very existence is unfortunate.

"No." Matthew shakes his head, as if he can banish the thought, and her. "No, now that Thom—I'm the last—"

"She is Grace's," says Hannah, and the idea snags inside Olivia, the thought that she could be somebody's, even if they are not here.

"But the bloodline," snarls Matthew. "My father said— Did you *know*?"

"No, of course not," says Hannah, but spoken words are clumsy things, and Olivia catches the snag in her voice, the higher pitch. She's lying. But Matthew hasn't noticed. He isn't listening.

"There must be some mistake," he says. "What has she told you?"

I'm right here, thinks Olivia. Her hands form the words, but he's treating her like a ghoul, something he can just ignore, so she reaches for the nearest breakable thing—a vase—and shoves it from the mantle.

It lands with a satisfying crash, shattering against the wooden floor, the sound loud enough to break Matthew from his rant. Then he rounds on her.

"You. Who are you really? Why did you come here?"

"She cannot speak," says Edgar.

"But she was invited," answers Hannah, holding up the letter.

"By whom?" demands Matthew, snatching the thin paper from her hand.

"Your father."

All the light goes out of him. All the heat, and the fury. In that instant, he looks young and frightened. And then his face slams shut, and he surges to the hearth and casts the letter into the fire.

Olivia lunges forward, but he forces her back as the paper

catches, burns. Her uncle's words to her gone up in smoke.

"Look at me," says Matthew, gripping her shoulders. His eyes, a lighter gray than hers and shot through with blue, are haunted. "My father did not send you that letter. He has been dead for more than a year."

Dead. The word rattles through her.

But it doesn't make sense. She closes her eyes, recalls the steady hand.

Come home, dear niece.

We cannot wait to welcome you.

"Matthew," coaxes Hannah. "Could he have written it before . . ."

"No," he bellows, the word as heavy as a door.

He scowls at Olivia, his hand tightening around her arm. He's thin and looks as though he hasn't slept a night in weeks, but there is something in his eyes that scares her.

"He said I was the last of them. He said there were no more." His voice splinters, as if in pain, but his fingers bite into her skin. "You cannot be here."

She twists free of his grip. Or perhaps he pushes her away. Either way, there is suddenly a stride's length between them, a narrow but uncrossable chasm. They stare across it.

"You should never have come to Gallant." He points to the door. "Go."

Olivia rocks back on her heels. Hannah and Edgar share a look.

"It's too dark now," says Edgar. "She cannot leave tonight."

Matthew swears under his breath. "At first light, then," he says, storming out. He calls back over his shoulder. "Get away from this house and never come back."

Olivia stares after him, angry and confused. She looks to Hannah and Edgar, hoping for some explanation, but neither speaks. The three of them stand there in the sitting room, silent save for the sound of Matthew's stomping boots, the crackling fire, Olivia's unsteady breath.

She stares into the flames, the letter gone, taking her dreams of Gallant with it. She looks to her suitcase, then to the door. Where is she supposed to go?

Hannah sighs. "No sense in worrying tonight. We'll sort it all out in the morning." She leans back against the sofa, and Edgar rests a hand on her arm. Olivia notices the way she leans into the touch. "I'm sorry," she says. "Matthew is not himself these days." Then, "He was a sweet boy, once."

Olivia has a hard time believing that. She tries to catch Edgar's eye, to ask what happened, but he won't look at her, so she kneels to pick up the pieces of the broken vase. Hannah shoos her away. "Leave that," she says, and then, with a small grin, "You did me a favor. I always thought it was ugly. Now," she says, shoving up to her feet again, "you must be hungry."

She isn't, really, but Hannah doesn't wait for an answer. "I'll go and see what I can rustle up," she says. "Edgar?"

"Come on, then, child," he says, lifting her case. "I'll show you to a room."

~~~

The stairs are old, but sturdy, their steps barely sounding as Edgar leads her up.

She catches his eye and signs. *How long have you been here?*

"Too long," he answers with a tired smile. Then, "Longer than Matthew, but not as long as Hannah."

Did you know my mother? she asks.

"I did. We were all heartbroken when she disappeared."

Olivia's heart quickens, her mother's words rising to her mind.

Free—a small word for such a magnificent thing.
I don't know what it feels like, but I want to find out.

Her mother wasn't stolen away from Gallant. She left this place on purpose. Olivia's hands move quickly, the questions spilling out.

Where did she go? Do you know why? Did she come back?

Edgar shakes his head, a slow and steady pendulum.

Is she dead?

That last question is the one she has always been afraid to ask, because the truth is, she does not know. Whenever she reads the final pages of the journal, she pictures her mother backing away toward the edge of a cliff. Step after step after step until the ground is gone and so is she.

There was a goodbye stitched into every word, and yet—

Is she dead? she asks again, because Edgar's head has

stopped moving. His shoulders rise. His face sags.

"I'm sorry," he says. "I don't know."

Frustration prickles through her, not at him, but at *her*, at *Grace*, the woman who vanished, leaving only a tattered notebook and a silent child on a stoop. At the way the story trails off, without the promise of an end.

They reach the upstairs landing, and Edgar leads her down a wide hall lined with doors, all of them closed.

"Ah, here we are," he says, stopping at the second on the left.

The door whispers open onto a beautiful room, larger than any of the matrons' quarters and twice as nice. Her eyes go to the bed—not a cot but a grand four-poster, pillows stuffed with down. Wide enough that she could fling out her arms and not touch the sides.

Edgar retreats, but not before Olivia signs *thank you.*

"For what?" he asks, and she gestures at the room, and the house, and herself before shrugging. *For everything.*

He nods, mustering a smile. "Hannah will be up shortly," he says, and then he's gone, drawing the door shut behind him.

Olivia stands there a moment, uncertain what to do. She has never had her own room, has always wondered how it would feel to have a space entirely hers, a door that she could close. And despite the strangeness of the scene downstairs, her cousin's cruelty and the questions mounting in her mind, she twirls across the floor and flings herself onto the bed. She expects to rouse a plume of dust, but there is none, only her limbs sinking into soft down. She lies there, arms spread like a snow angel.

My room, she thinks, before reminding herself that it is only hers for the night.

She sits up and looks around, taking stock. There is an elegant wardrobe, and an ottoman, and a desk before a large window, the shutters latched. Across the room there's a second door, and she opens it expecting to find a closet, or perhaps another hall, but it is a bathroom, a glorious space with a mirror and a sink and a claw-foot tub. Not a steel drum and a foot of tepid water but a massive porcelain bath, large enough to soak in.

There are no other girls elbowing their way to the sink, taking up the hot water and shouldering her so they can do their hair, examine their faces, so she lingers, studying her reflection, as she has so many times, scouring it the way she does her mother's journal, searching for clues about who she is, where she came from.

Here are her eyes, slate gray. Her skin, pale but not porcelain. Her hair, the almost-black of charcoal.

Olivia notices a small hair comb on the counter, the spine patterned with blue flowers. She runs her fingers over the delicate tines, then takes up the comb and fastens it above her ear. The blue flowers are bright against her hair, which hangs dead straight and just long enough to skim her shoulders. She cut it that spring, in a fit of pique. She hated the solemn plaits the girls at Merilance were forced to wear, so she stole a pair of sewing shears and cut it to her collar, just short enough to make the braids impossible. She smiles a little whenever she thinks of the look on Matron Agatha's face, the impotent rage.

She tugs the comb free, returns it to its place, and decides to run herself a bath.

The water, when it spills out, is hot and clear, steam rising to her fingers.

She strips and climbs in, savoring the almost painful heat. A trio of elegant bottles lines the wall beside the tub, all of them half full. The stoppers are stiff, and as she fights to open one, it slips and tumbles into the basin. In seconds, there are scented bubbles everywhere, and she laughs, a soft breathy sound, at the absurdity of this, of a day begun peeling potatoes at Merilance and ended here, in a house with no uncle and a boy who does not want her there, in a tub full of lavender soap.

She sinks under the surface, where the world is quiet and dark, taps on the side of the tub, the sound echoing softly all around. Like rain against the roof of a garden shed. She stays until the water goes tepid, until her skin prunes, and even then, she's only drawn out by the promise of supper and the waiting bed.

She rises, thoughts thick and limbs heavy, wrapping herself in a plush white towel. The steam melts from the mirror, and it's probably just the heat of the bath, but her cheeks look brighter, her skin less pale, as if she left her old self like a soap line in the tub.

Her clothes sit piled on the floor. A heap of gray cloth. She wants to burn them, but they are all she has, so she opens the wardrobe, intending to throw them in. And stops.

A few empty hangers dot the rack, but the rest are draped with dresses. Her fingers trail over cotton and wool and silk. A few have been eaten at by moths, the knitting loosened by time, but they are still nicer than anything she's ever touched. It is obvious that the room once belonged to someone else, just as obvious that she is gone, though it's strange that she left so many things behind. Stranger still that her room has been left intact, untouched—the bottles by the tub, the hair comb by the sink, the clothes in the cupboard—as if any day she might come back.

In a drawer, Olivia finds a cream nightgown. It is too long, too large, but she doesn't care. The fabric is soft and warm against her skin, and she lets it swallow her up.

She didn't hear Hannah come in, but a neat little tea tray sits waiting on the ottoman. A bowl of stew. A slice of bread. A pat of butter. And a peach. A little gold key now juts out of the lock in the door. She presses her ear to the wood as she turns it, listens to the satisfying click, the marvelous weight of the metal in her hand. The luxury of a closed door.

The stew is hearty and hot, the bread crusty but soft inside, the fruit perfectly sweet, and when she's done, she falls into bed, sure that she has never been so clean or so comfortable.

You are wanted. You are needed. You belong with us.

She wraps the words around her, tries to hold them close,

but as her body sinks into the sheets, so do her spirits, until all she can hear is Matthew's voice.

My father did not send that letter, he said, feeding the paper to the flames.

But if Arthur Prior did not write to her, who *did*?

l am afraid it wasn't my hand on her cheek
wasn't my voice in my mouth
wasn't my eyes watching her sleep

Chapter Six

Olivia cannot sleep.

The house has too much space and too few sounds to fill it. There are no city noises here, no squeaking springs. No matrons shuffling up and down the halls, no clatter of the streets beyond. Instead of the sleeping and wheezing and sighing of two dozen girls, there is only her own breath, her own movement in the too-big bed.

And so she lies awake, her mother's journal pressed to her chest as she listens, straining to find the melody of Gallant.

Olivia spent years learning the notes that made up Merilance, the shuffle of socked feet, the sleep-thick murmurs in the middle of the night, the whistle and pop of the radiators, the tap of the head matron's cane on the wooden floor as she crossed the house.

Here, inside her borrowed room, she hears—nothing.

Earlier, she heard Hannah and Edgar moving about, their voices little more than highs and lows through the halls. She heard a door slam—and guessed that it was Matthew. But now it is late, and all the noises have settled, leaving only a muffled silence, the walls too thick, the night kept out by locks and shutters.

Olivia cannot bear the quiet. She strikes a match, eliciting a satisfying crack as light blossoms, pushing back the dark. Something twitches at the corner of her sight, but it is only the small flame dancing on the walls.

She lights a taper and opens her mother's book to read, even though she knows the words by heart.

I had a bird once. I kept it in a cage. But one day someone let it go. I was so angry, then, but now I wonder if it was me. If I rose in the night, half-asleep, and slipped the lock and set it free.

Free—a small word for such a magnificent thing.

As she reads, she lets her fingers wander over the strange drawings. In the unsteady light, her eyes play tricks on her, twisting the blooms of ink until they seem like they're moving.

She doesn't like to linger on the later entries, the darker ones, so she pages past them, catching only fragments.

. . . I slept in your ashes last night . . . It was never this quiet . . . His voice in your mouth . . . I want to go home . . .

Until all at once, it stops. The jagged writing drops away,

leaving only empty space, blank pages stretching to the very last page, where the letter waits.

Olivia Olivia Olivia

Her gaze drops to the bottom of the page.

You will be safe as long as you stay away from Gallant

She squints at the word, for years a mystery—still a mystery. She flings off the covers and gets to her feet.

For so long, Gallant was nothing but that word, the last one her mother ever wrote. Now she knows it is a place, and she is *here*, and if she is not allowed to stay beyond the night, well then, she wants to see as much of it as possible. To learn the contours of the house where her mother lived, as if knowing one will help explain the other.

The key turns with a click, and she steps silently into the hall. Every other room is dark, save one, a narrow strip of light beneath the door. She shields her candle and sets out, slipping barefoot down the hall.

Olivia has always relished sound, but she knows how to be quiet.

Some nights, back at Merilance, she'd creep out of bed and wander through the darkened house, pretend it was a kind of conquest. She'd twirl down the empty halls, just because she could. Count the steps from one side to the other, fog the windows with her breath and draw shapes in the steam, the only witness the ghoul that sat on the stairs and peered at her between the railings.

There, in the dark, she could pretend the place was hers.

But for all she tried, the grim gray building never played its part. It was too cold, too hollow, too much itself, and every night when she climbed back into bed, she was reminded that Merilance was a house, but it would never be a home.

She tells herself that Gallant won't be one either, not if Matthew has his way, and yet, as she makes her way down the stairs, the polished banister beneath her palm, it all feels so— familiar. With every silent step, the house leans in and whispers *hello*, whispers *welcome*, whispers *home*.

She retraces her steps, crossing the foyer to the sitting room, the fire nothing but a handful of ticking embers now, the broken vase swept up from the floor. From there, she wanders deeper into the heart of the house. She discovers a dining room, the table long enough to seat a dozen; a lounge with furniture that looks untouched; a kitchen, still warm.

As Olivia crosses the house, the candle wavers, and so does her shadow. When she shifts the light from hand to hand, it leaps unsteadily around her, so it takes her a moment to realize she is not alone.

The ghoul stands halfway down the hall.

A woman—or at least, the pieces of her, hanging in the air

like smoke. A curtain of dark hair. A narrow shoulder. A hand, drifting out as if to touch her.

Olivia jerks backward in surprise, expecting the ghoul to disappear. It doesn't. Instead, it turns its back on her and moves swiftly down the hall, drifting in and out of sight like a body between lamplights.

Wait, she thinks, as it plunges away from her, as it reaches the door at the end and passes straight through. Olivia hurries after it, feet pounding across the rug, candle nearly guttering as she throws the door open onto shallow darkness. As she steps inside, the taper reveals a study, high-ceilinged and windowless. She turns, searching the corners, but the ghoul is gone.

Olivia lets out an unsteady breath. She always wondered if the things she saw were bound to Merilance. Whether the building was haunted, or she was. Apparently, it wasn't the school. She turns to go, and the candle wavers in her hand, light dancing over bookshelves, a dark wood desk, before catching on the curve of metal resting there.

Olivia frowns, stepping toward the strange shape, nearly as tall as she is.

If there is a word for it, she doesn't know.

It looks mechanical. Half clock and half sculpture. A kind of . . . orb, made of concentric rings, each set at a different angle. Up close, she sees that there are two houses set inside the piece, each one balanced on its own metal ring.

Her fingers twitch. She cannot shake the feeling that the

slightest push would set the whole thing off balance and bring the model crashing to the floor. And yet, she cannot help herself. Her hand drifts up, and—

The door groans behind her.

Olivia turns, too fast, and the candle in her hand goes out, plunging the room into black.

Fear grips her, sudden and sharp. She abandons the study, blinking furiously, willing her eyes to adjust. But the shutters are all latched, and the darkness in the house is thick as syrup. She feels her way back down the hall, reminding herself she is not afraid of the dark, even though she has never known a dark like this. The house seems to grow around her, the hallways branching, multiplying, until she is sure she is lost.

And then, to her right, her vision lifts, the darkness thinning until she can just make out the edges of the space. Somewhere, there is a light. Not bright, but watery and white. She turns down a narrow hall and finds another, smaller foyer. And there, at the back of it, a door.

There are two kinds of doors in a house.

The kind that lead from room to room, and the kind that lead from inside to out—and this is one of those. Thin light spills through a small glass pane set into the wood. She has to stand on her toes to see through the window, and when she does, she finds a crescent moon hanging in the sky, showering the garden below in strands of silver.

The garden. The one she first glimpsed when the car pulled

around the drive, the promise of something lovely tucked behind the house.

Even in the dark, it is a sight. Trees and trellised roses, gravel paths and groomed flowers and a carpet of grass. She wants to throw the door open and spill out into the night, wants to walk barefoot through the blades, wants to feel the velvet petals of the roses, lie on a bench beneath the moon, wants to breathe in the beauty before she is sent away.

She tries the door, but it is locked.

Olivia pats the pockets of her nightgown, wishing she'd brought her set of picks. But then she feels the gold key that fit her bedroom door. It's a simple shape, little more than a W. And in a house with so many doors, would you really want more than one key? Olivia slides it into the lock and holds her breath and turns, expecting resistance. Instead, she feels the satisfying *thunk* of a bolt sliding free.

The handle is cool under her touch, and when she turns the knob, the door sighs open, just a crack, carrying cool night air and—

A man surges out of the dark.

He comes straight through the wooden door and into the foyer. Half his face is missing, and Olivia staggers back, away from the door and the man who is not a man at all but a ghoul. It scowls at her with one eye, a stained hand thrust out, not in welcome, but in warning. It cannot touch her, she tells herself, it isn't *there*, but when it stomps forward, fingers curling into fists, she turns and runs blindly through the dark, somehow finds her way back to the staircase and the upstairs hall and her bedroom door, pulling it shut behind her.

And even though it's only wood, she feels safer with it closed.

Olivia's heart pounds in her ears as she climbs under the covers, pulling her mother's journal to her like a shield. She has never been afraid of the dark, but tonight, she relights the lamp. As she sits, her back to the headboard and her eyes on the shadows, she realizes—

She left the key in the door downstairs.

Chapter Seven

Olivia doesn't remember falling asleep.

She doesn't remember getting up either, but she must have, because it's morning, and she's sitting at the little desk before the window. The shutters have been flung wide, and sunlight streams in, warm and bright where it falls on the desk, on her hands, on the journal there, the gilded *G* pressed into the cover. Her mother's book, and yet, this one is different. It's red where hers was green, and there are no twin lines gouged into the cover, and when she turns through the pages, the writing blurs, dissolving every time she tries to read it.

She squints, trying to make sense of it, sure that the letters are about to come together.

A hand comes to rest on her shoulder, the touch gentle and warm, but when she turns her head to look, it is rotting, bone visible through ruined skin.

Olivia sits up with a gasp.

She is still in bed. The shutters are latched, thin light seeping round the edges. Her heart pounds and her head spins and it takes her a moment to realize what that was: a *dream*. It is already slipping through her fingers, the details going thin, and she presses her palms against her eyes and tries to remember. Not the ghoulish hand, but the journal.

Olivia flings off the bedsheets and goes to the desk, half expecting to find the red book waiting on top, but it's not there. Her gaze drops to the drawer in the front of the desk, the little keyhole like a spot of ink. When she pulls, the drawer resists, but it's a silly excuse for a lock, and it takes only a hairpin and a handful of seconds to get it open.

Inside, she finds a pincushion stuck with needles. A small embroidery hoop, half-formed poppies in the center of pale cloth. A pot of ink, a handful of sketches on loose paper, and a few sheets of stationery, embossed with two elegant letters: *GP*.

Grace Prior.

Of course. This was her mother's room.

Olivia runs her hand over the desk, the wood worn smooth with age. A strange urge washes over her, and she goes back to the bed, turning through the rumpled sheets until she finds the journal she's always had, with its dented green cover. She sets it gently on the desk. There is no groove for it, no outline where the sun has bleached the wood, and yet, it *fits*. The pretty green book, so out of place at Merilance, belongs here, blends right in, like drawings made by the same hand.

Olivia pulls out the chair and sits in her mother's shadow, hands resting lightly on the cover. The dream drifts back to her, and she closes her eyes and tries to conjure more before it slips away.

Knuckles rap on the door, and she jumps. She slides the journal into the drawer like a secret and gets to her feet just as Hannah sweeps in like a gust of wind, a tea tray balanced on one hip.

"The house gets cold in the morning," she says brightly. "Thought you could do with a little warming up."

Olivia nods in thanks and steps aside as Hannah deposits the tray on the desk and reaches up to free the latch. The shutters fall open, filling the room with fresh air and streaks of sun. And then, Hannah draws the gold key from her pocket and sets it on the desk. Olivia winces at the sight of it, the reproach of the metal dropping onto wood.

"You *mustn't* go out in the dark," says Hannah, and the way she says it, it's like she's reciting a rule.

There were a great many rules back at Merilance. Most of them felt hollow, pointless, concocted just to show the matrons' control. But there is real worry in Hannah's eyes, so Olivia nods, even though she will not be here another night.

With the shutters thrown back, Olivia realizes her room is at the front of the house, the window looking out onto the drive, the ribbon of road and the distant iron arch proclaiming GALLANT. She looks down, but there is no car waiting to take her back to Merilance, only the fountain and the pale stone woman standing at its center.

Hannah's gaze drops to the desk drawer, the hairpin still jutting from the lock. Olivia holds her breath, braced for the rebuke, but the woman only chuckles, soft and honest. "Your mother was a curious girl, too."

Olivia remembers then, what Edgar said, that Hannah had been here the longest, and the woman must be able to see the question as it scrawls across Olivia's face, because she nods and says, "Yes. I knew Grace."

Grace, Grace, Grace. The name unravels through her mind.

"Matthew doesn't remember her," continues Hannah. "He was still a child when she left, but I was here when she was born. I was here when she ran away. The whole house, what was left of it, waited, but I knew she wasn't coming back."

Tell me, Olivia signs, hoping Hannah can read the longing in her eyes if not her hands. *Tell me everything.*

The woman sinks into the chair, looking suddenly tired. She runs a hand through her hair, and Olivia sees the threads of gray stealing through the mess of brown curls. She pours her a cup of tea, but Hannah only chuckles and nods for her to drink. Olivia brings it to her lips. It tastes like mint, and honey, and spring, and she wraps her fingers around the cup as Hannah speaks.

"When I first saw you, on the steps, I thought you were a ghost."

Olivia gestures down at her pale limbs, but Hannah smiles and shakes her head. "No, not like that. It's only, you look just like her. Your mother. Grace was a willful child. A clever girl. But she was always restless here." Hannah laces her fingers in her lap. "Her own mother left when she was young, and her father took ill when she was just about your age, and died within the year. Her older brother, Arthur, was away, and that year, your mother and I, we had the whole house to ourselves. So much space, and yet, she was always looking for more. Always wandering. Always searching."

I had a bird once. I kept it in a cage.

"She was such a handful, your mother, and the house was too big for the two of us, so I hired Edgar to help. And then Arthur came back with a lovely girl—Isabelle, that was her name—and they married in the garden. I made the cake myself. Matthew was born, and then Thomas was on the way and—"

She swallows suddenly, as if she can take those last words back.

"Well," she says, "it was a happy time. But even then, Grace had one eye on the door."

But one day someone let it go.

"Arthur was steady, but she was smoke, always looking for a way out." Hannah's gaze drifts around the room. "I came in here one morning, and she was gone. The shutters were thrown, and the window was open, as if she'd flown away."

Olivia looks to the window.

Now I wonder if it was me.

Hannah clears her throat. "You may blame her for leaving,

but I never could. This is not an easy place to live."

Neither was Merilance, thinks Olivia darkly. She would have chosen Gallant any day, if anyone had asked. This place is a palace. This place is a dream.

Hannah looks up, studying Olivia's face. "She wrote to me, once. Before you were born. Wouldn't say where she was or where she was going. Wouldn't say anything about your father, but I knew something was wrong. I could see it in the way she wrote."

Hannah trails off, and Olivia can see a shine in her eyes, the warning of tears.

I grow wide, but you grow thinner by the day. I can see you withering. I am afraid tomorrow I will see straight through you. I am afraid the next, you will be gone.

"She didn't say goodbye, but I saw the end in every word, and I knew—I just *knew*—something had happened."

A single tear escapes down the woman's weathered cheek.

"I worried, after, about you both. And when she didn't write again, I feared the worst for Grace. But I had a feeling that you were out there. Perhaps it was just a hope. I began to make a list of places you might be, if you'd even been born, if she'd chosen to take you somewhere. But in the end, I couldn't—that is, I never tried to find you."

But someone did. Someone called her home.

"I think part of me hoped that you were somewhere safe."

That word again—safe. But what is *safe*? Tombs are *safe*. Merilance was *safe*. *Safe* does not mean happy, does not mean well, does not mean kind.

"I've watched so many Priors wither here," Hannah mutters to herself. "All to guard that blasted gate."

Olivia frowns. She touches Hannah's hand, and the woman startles, coming back to herself. "I'm so sorry," she says, wiping the tears from her cheek and rising to her feet. "And here I just came to tell you there's a pot of porridge on the stove."

Olivia stares at Hannah as she hurries away, a hundred questions tangled in her head. Halfway to the door the woman stops, one hand diving back into her pocket. "Oh, I almost forgot," she says, "I found this downstairs. I thought you might like it."

She draws out a card the size of her palm and turns it toward Olivia, who stiffens at the image there. It is a portrait. A young woman's face, looking off to one side. It could be a picture of *her*, in several years' time, if the hair were darker, the chin a bit more pointed. But the look in the eyes is hers—all mischief—and she realizes two things.

That she's looking at an image of her mother.

And that she's seen her before.

Or rather, pieces of her, floating in the hall downstairs.

Which means that Hannah is right, and wrong. Her mother is never coming home.

She is already here.

Stay with me. Stay with me. Stay with me. I would write the words a thousand times if they'd be strong enough to hold you here.

Chapter Eight

Grace Prior is dead.

After all those years, Olivia knew her mother wasn't coming back. And yet, there was always that narrow sliver of hope. Like a door left ajar. Now it swings shut.

She sinks onto the ottoman, the portrait in her hands.

What happened to you? she wonders, consulting the image as if it's not static, a collection of lines and oil paint. As if it can tell her anything.

Why did you leave? she asks, knowing she means both Gallant and herself. But the girl in the portrait only looks away, as if distracted, already planning her escape.

Olivia blows out an exasperated breath. She'd have more luck, she thinks, asking the ghoul. Perhaps she *will*. She rises, setting the portrait on the desk, and starts toward the door, only to pass a mirror and realize she's still in her nightgown.

Yesterday's dress sits on the floor, drab, discarded. Her suitcase lies open, the second gray shift waiting there. These clothes belong to someone else, a student at Merilance, an orphan in a garden shed. Olivia cannot bring herself to put that life back on, to feel it against her skin.

She goes to the wardrobe and studies the dresses still hanging inside, trying to reconstruct her mother from swatches of fabric, to shape the image of a woman she has never known. They are all too large on Olivia, but not by much. A few inches spread across a body. A few years between. How old was Grace when she left? Eighteen? Twenty?

Olivia picks out a butter-yellow dress and a pair of flats, a size too large. Her heels slip out with every step, making her feel like a child playing dress-up in her mother's clothes. Which, she supposes, is exactly what she is. She sighs and kicks off the shoes, resolving to go barefoot as she takes up her sketchpad and sets off in search of answers.

Gallant is a different place in daylight.

The shutters are open, the windows flung wide, the shadows retreating as daylight spills in and a cool breeze drives the stale air from the massive house. But the sun has lifted a veil, and she can see that the house is not *quite* so grand as she first thought. Gallant is an old estate, fighting the fall into disrepair, an elegant figure beginning to droop. Skin sagging a little over bones.

On the stairs, she stops and peers down at the foyer floor. She did not see it in the dark, but now, from up here, the inlaid pattern resolves into a series of concentric circles, each one tipped at its own angle. It reminds her, instantly, of the object she found in the study. The tilted metal rings around the model of the house. Houses. There were two.

As she continues down the stairs, sounds rise up to meet her.

The low murmur of voices, the metal scrape of a spoon against a bowl. Her stomach growls, but as she nears the kitchen, the voices draw tighter into strings of speech.

"Is it really a kindness, to keep her here?" asks Edgar.

"She has nowhere to go," answers Hannah.

"She can go back to the school."

Olivia's hands tighten on the sketchpad. Defiance blooms inside her chest. She will *not* go back to Merilance. That is a past, not a future.

"And if they will not take her?"

Olivia backs away from the kitchen.

"She doesn't know what it means, to be a Prior. To be here."

"Then we must tell her."

Her bare feet stop. She hovers, ears pricked, but then Edgar sighs and says, "It is Matthew's choice, not ours. He is the master of the house." And at that, she rolls her eyes and turns away. Five minutes with her cousin, and he made it clear, she is not welcome here. She doubts he means to tell her why.

If she wants to know, she'll have to find the truth herself.

Olivia continues down one hall and up another, the walls here lined with family portraits. Paintings run the length of the hall, and the faces in them ripple and age, going from children in one portrait, to adults in the next, to parents with their own family in the third.

Small plaques mounted to the base of every frame announce the people in them.

It begins with Alexander Prior, a stoic man in a high-collared coat, Matthew's same gray-blue eyes leveled on her. There is Maryanne Prior, a sturdy woman, broad-shouldered and proud, the ghost of a smile tugging at her lips. There is Jacob and Evelyn. Alice and Paul.

It is so strange, to see her face reflected, distorted, echoed in so many others. Here is the line of her cheek and the curve of her mouth. Here is the angle of her eye and the slope of her nose. The details scattered like seeds across the portraits. She has never had a family, and now she has a tree.

You are one of us, they seem to say. Olivia studies their faces—she has drawn her own a dozen times, searching for clues, but now, among so many Priors, she can begin to separate her features and find the ones that do not fit, the details that must have been her father's. Her black hair, for one, and the pallor of her skin, and the exact color of her eyes, not gray-blue, like Matthew's, or gray-green like her mother's, but the flat untinted gray of slate, of smoke. A charcoal sketch among the oil paintings.

She passes whole generations of Priors before she finds her mother's face again, even younger here, sitting on a bench beside a boy who looks like Matthew, the same tawny hair, the same deep-set eyes. She realizes it must be her uncle, Arthur, even before she sees the plaque.

In the next portrait, he is full-grown, and she realizes, she has seen him before, right here, in the house. What's left of him, at least. Half a face, an outstretched hand, a body barging through the garden door. The ghoul she met last night. The one who kept her from the garden.

In the portrait, he is hale and hearty, one hand on a garden trellis and the other wrapped around his wife, Isabelle. She's thin as a willow, her gaze off to one side, as if she already knows she will leave.

After that should be Matthew, but the wall is bare, as if still waiting for the next portrait to be hung. And yet, when she steps closer, she can see the ghost of one, the wallpaper a slightly different color, and higher up, the small hole where a nail was driven in. She draws her palm over the bare wall and wonders why her cousin is missing.

A door sits at the other end of the hall, and she moves toward it, hoping it's the study she found the night before, the one with the strange sculpture on the desk. But when the handle turns, the door falls open onto a different room.

Heavy curtains have been drawn across a window, but they do not meet, and in the break between them, a ribbon of sunlight spills through the room, onto the glossy black body of a piano.

Olivia's fingers twitch at the sight of it.

There was a piano back at Merilance, an ancient thing shoved up against one wall. For a few years, the sound would wander through the halls, the awkward melody of someone learning, stiffly pecking out the notes. The girls shuffled through like cards, Matron Agatha impatient to see if any were worth the work.

Olivia was seven when it was finally her turn.

She couldn't wait. Drawing had come so naturally, as if her hands were shaped to the task, a direct line between her eyes and her pencil. And the piano might have been the same. The joy she'd felt at those first ringing notes. The thrill of commanding such sound. The thunder of the low keys, the kettle whistle of the high. Each and every one its own mood, its own message, a language played out in C and G and E.

Her hands wanted to race ahead, but the matron tsked in warning, rapping her knuckles every time her fingers strayed from scales.

Olivia had lost her temper then and slammed the lid down over the keys, nearly clipping the matron's hand. She *hadn't*, of course, but it didn't matter. She was dismissed, those few spare notes still ringing in her ears.

Anger had pooled in her stomach, rising every time she heard another girl clumsily tapping out the notes, until one night she'd slipped out of bed and into the room where the piano was kept, a pair of cutters in one hand. She'd pried up the lid, revealing the delicate body of wires and hammers that made the music from the keys. Keys she couldn't touch.

They reminded her of the diagram in the old anatomy text, the muscles and tendons of the throat laid bare. Cut here to silence a voice.

She couldn't do it.

In the end, it didn't matter. Arthritis soon crept into Agatha's hands, and the lessons were abandoned. The piano sat untouched until the wires loosened and the notes all fell out of key. But Olivia always longed to play.

Now she drifts forward into the shaft of sunlight, creeping softly toward the instrument, as if it might wake. It lies still, teeth hidden beneath the onyx lid. She eases it back, exposing the pattern of black and white, the shine worn to matte with use, faint indents in the ivory. Her right hand hovers, then comes to rest on the keys. They are cool beneath her fingers. She presses down, plays a single note. It carries softly through the room, and Olivia cannot help but smile.

She traces her way up the scale. And as she hits the highest note—

Something moves.

Not in the room with her, but beyond, glimpsed in the gap between the curtains.

She steps past the piano and pulls the curtain aside, revealing a giant bay window, the bench lined with pillows, and beyond the glass, the garden.

Olivia Prior has dreamed of gardens. Every grim gray month at Merilance, she longed for carpets of grass, for riotous blooms, for a world engulfed in color. And here it is. Last night it was a moonlit tangle of hedge and vine. Now it is sun-drenched, stunning, a field of green interrupted everywhere by red, gold, violet, white.

There is a vegetable patch to one side, rows of leeks and carrots rising from the soil, and a copse of pale trees to the other, their branches dotted pink and green. An orchard. And then, her gaze drifts past it all, beyond the trellised roses and down the soft green slope, to a wall.

Or at least, the remains of one, a ruined stretch of stone, its edges crumbling, its front threaded over with ivy.

Another shudder of motion draws her attention back to the garden. Matthew is kneeling, head bowed, before a line of roses. As she watches, he straightens and turns, shielding his eyes as he looks up at the house. At her. Even from here, she can see the frown sweep like a shadow across his face. Olivia backs away from the glass. But she is not retreating.

It takes a few minutes and two wrong turns, but she finds the second foyer again, and the garden door. The one she unlocked the night before. There's something on the floor, a dark residue, as if someone's tracked dirt into the house, but when she bends to touch it, she feels nothing. As if the stain has pressed itself straight into the stone. She remembers the ghoul, forcing her back, his hand thrust out. But there is no one to stop her now, and the door is no longer locked. It swings open at her touch, and she inches around the odd shadow on the floor.

And steps out into the sun.

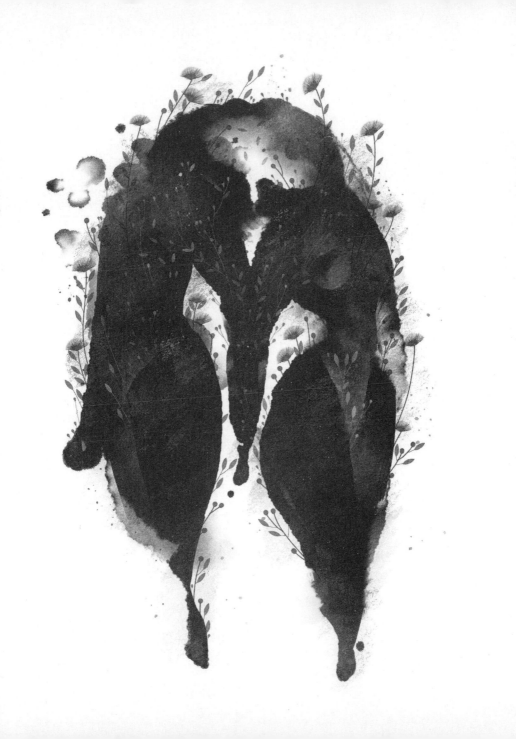

Chapter Nine

The first things Olivia learned to draw were flowers.

It would have been easier, of course, to draw pots and hearths, dining benches and sleeping cots, things she saw every day. But Olivia filled the pages of her first sketchbook with flowers. The silk ones she saw every time she was sent to the head matron's office. The stubborn yellow weeds that forced their way up here and there between the gravel. The roses she saw in a book. But sometimes, she'd invent her own. Fill the corners of every page with strange and wild blooms, conjuring whole gardens out of empty space, each more expansive than the last.

But none of them were real.

For all her skill, she couldn't wander through them as she does now, couldn't feel the grass beneath her feet, the soft petals tickling her palm. Olivia smiles, the sunlight warm against her skin.

She passes beneath a trellised arch, draws her hand along a waist-high hedge. She never knew there were so many different kinds of roses, so many different sizes or shades, and she doesn't know the names for any of them.

She sinks onto a sun-soaked bench, the sketchpad open on her knee, her fingers itching to capture every detail.

But her eyes keep drifting to the garden wall.

It sits, watching from the distance, and she knows that is a strange verb, *watch*, a human word, but that is how it feels. As if it's staring at her.

Her pencil whispers over the paper, the gestures swift and sure as she finds the outline of the wall. It is more of a ruin, really, as if a stone house once stood there on the site, but has since fallen down, leaving only a single side. Or perhaps a wall once surrounded the estate. She looks around for other ruins, but the rest is rolling green. Gallant sits in a basin, surrounded by open pasture and distant hills. A wall seems rather pointless in a place like this.

Olivia finishes her drawing, and frowns. It isn't right.

She studies the two walls, one on paper and the other on grass, searching for her mistakes, some wrong angle or misplaced line, but she cannot find it. So she turns the page and tries again. She starts at the edges and works in, finding the outline.

"Why are you still here?"

Matthew trudges toward her, a bucket hanging from one hand, and she braces for a tirade or a tantrum, holds her breath and waits for him to order her away, drag her through the house and out onto the steps like a piece of misplaced luggage. But he doesn't, just crouches at the edge of a planting.

She studies him, watching as he runs his gloved hands through the rose bushes, the gesture almost gentle as he peels apart the thorny limbs, searching for weeds.

How strange, to think that they are cousins.

That yesterday she was alone.

And today she is not.

All her life, she has wanted a house and a garden and a room of her own. But tucked inside that want was something else: a family. Parents who smothered her with love. Siblings who teased because they cared. Grandparents, aunts and uncles, nieces and nephews—in her mind a family was a sprawling thing, an orchard full of roots and branches.

Instead she has been given this single, scowling tree.

Her pencil scratches, carving the lines of him. In daylight, the resemblance is obvious in the width of his brow, the slope of his cheek—but so are the differences. His eyes are bluer in the light, his hair a warmer shade, the light brown shot through with gold. The three or four years that have given him height and breadth, the difference between a plant left to scrounge for sun and one clearly nurtured. And yet, there is something worn about him, thin. It's in the way he's shaded, the shadows under his eyes, the hollows in his cheeks. He looks as though he hasn't slept in weeks.

Matthew works slowly, methodically, pulling each intrusive weed and dropping it in a basket. She reaches out, runs her fingers over the velvet petals, leans in to sniff, expecting . . . she isn't sure. Perfume? But the flowers hardly smell at all.

"They're grown for color, not for scent," he says, pulling up another weed. This time she notices how pale it is. Perhaps it only seems that way, against the too-bright reds and pinks and golds of the garden. But in his hand the tendril looks completely gray, devoid of color.

He unwinds another weed from the stem of a rose and rips it free, dropping the strange intruder into the bucket.

"They run beneath the soil," he says. "Push up and strangle everything."

He glances at her as he says it, and she signs, as quickly as she can:

What happened to my uncle?

Matthew frowns. She tries again, slower, but he shakes his head. "You can flap your hands all you like," he says. "I don't know what you're saying."

Olivia grits her teeth and turns to a fresh page in her sketch-book, writing the question out in quick and sloping cursive. But when she holds the page up toward him, he is no longer looking. He is on his feet again, walking away toward another row of roses. Olivia hisses through her teeth and follows.

A few steps, and then he turns on her, his eyes fever bright.

"Edgar says you cannot speak. Are you deaf as well?"

Olivia scowls in answer.

"Good," he says. "Then listen close. You need to leave."

She shakes her head. How can he understand? This place is

paradise compared to where she was. Besides, this was her mother's home. Just because Grace left, why must Olivia? She is a Prior, too, after all.

"Do you know *anything* about this house?" He steps toward her as he speaks. She doesn't step back. "This place is cursed. *We* are cursed." There is more than anger in Matthew's eyes—there's fear. "To be a Prior is to live and die on these grounds, driven mad by ghosts."

Is it the ghouls that scare him? She wants to tell him she is not afraid. That she has been haunted all her life. It will take more than ghouls to make her go. But he turns away, shaking his head.

"I have lost so much," he says under his breath. "I will not let it be for nothing, all because a foolish girl didn't have the sense to stay away."

"Fine day, isn't it?" calls Hannah, coming toward them down the path, her wild curls pulled up in a messy bun. "First bit of warmth we've had in weeks."

Matthew sighs, rubbing his eyes. "Have you called for a car?"

Hannah's gaze flicks to Olivia's, a question there. *Do you want the car to come?* And for all that Matthew's said, and all he's choosing not to say, she doesn't want to go. She is not afraid of ghosts. But she is afraid of where that car might take her.

Olivia shakes her head, and Hannah answers, "No word yet, I'm afraid." A pail swings from one strong hand, filled with the soft gray pulp of mortar. "Edgar saw a few more cracks," she says, and Matthew's attention goes to the garden wall. He stands, holding out his hand for the pail. She hesitates.

"I don't mind helping," she says. "You could do with some rest."

"You'll have to do without me soon enough."

Hannah winces, as if struck. "Matthew," she says, "I wish you wouldn't talk like that."

But he waves the words away and takes the pail. "I can manage," he says, turning toward the wall. Olivia moves to follow, but he shakes his head and points to the ground between them.

"You stay put," he says, as if she is a troublesome pet. But he must be able to tell she has no plans of sitting still, because he nods at the bucket he left beside the roses. "If you want to help, keep pulling weeds." He pulls off his gloves and offers them to her. "And stay away from the wall." He turns and trudges down the slope.

Hannah tries to smile, but it is half a grimace and doesn't touch her eyes as they land on Olivia's borrowed dress. "Mind the thorns," she says, retreating up the path.

Olivia sets her sketchpad on the bench and tugs on the gloves. She doesn't mind the task. The sun warms the air, and when she crouches, the low world smells of soil and bloom. She starts where Matthew stopped, and it doesn't take long to find the first weed, a coil reaching up to strangle a bright pink blossom.

Olivia pries it free, and holds the tendril to the light.

It's strange, thin and spined and the color of ash. Back at

Merilance, everything felt like it was rendered in shades of gray, but now she realizes that wasn't really true. The colors were there, just faded, washed-out versions of themselves, but this—this is a graphite sketch against a watercolor scene.

Olivia continues down the row, working her way along the path until she hits the end of the rose bed. She glances down the sloping garden to the wall, where Matthew kneels, smoothing mortar into half a dozen cracks. It seems pointless to mend the wall, when it is clearly falling down.

The sun is high now, and the shade of the orchard beckons. She drifts away from the roses and into the copse of trees, scanning the ground for weeds or fallen fruit. But something else draws her eye. Beyond the orchard, a cluster of short pale shapes. At first glance, she thinks they must be stumps, but then the sun strikes stone, and she realizes they are graves.

It is a field of Priors, interrupted here and there by other names. The latest grave belongs to Matthew's father, Arthur. Buried here last fall. Nearby a pair of legs stretch out, ankles crossed. Shoulders slumped forward. A head, mostly missing. A ghoul. Olivia hurries toward it, hoping it will be her mother, but when the ruined face looks up, it belongs to a man. Not the one who blocked her way the night before, but another, older.

The ghoul glares at Olivia with what's left of its face and points a half-formed hand toward the house. A chill rolls over her and she retreats, away from the graveyard and the orchard and back into the sunlit garden.

Down by the wall, Matthew is upright, studying his work, wiping his forehead with the back of his arm. The day is warm, and her hands are sweating in the too-big gloves. She tugs them off and wanders back toward the bench where she left her sketchpad.

But as she bends to pick it up, she sees a gray stem pushing up through the soil, twining round the bench's leg. Olivia takes hold of the weed and pulls, but it is stubborn and strong. She tugs harder, her palm prickling where it meets the tendril. And then, too late, she feels it *move*.

A quick, sharp jerk, followed by the rake of heat across her palm. Olivia winces and drops the weed, looking down at her hand, where the spines have sliced a narrow line. Blood wells on her skin.

She looks around for somewhere to wipe it. If she were wearing her own gray shift instead of her mother's yellow dress, she would use the hem, but she can't bring herself to stain the soft cotton, so she kneels to wipe the blood on the grass when a hand comes out of nowhere, closing like a cage around her wrist.

"Stop," snaps Matthew, wrenching her upright. He sees the blood streaked across her palm, and pales.

"What have you done?" he asks, and there's no kindness in his voice, no care. If anything, he seems mad at her. She gestures down at the stubborn weed, the one that cut her.

But it isn't there.

Matthew produces a kerchief, and binds it tight around her

weeping palm, as if it were a mortal wound.

"Get inside," he orders, pointing at the house, an echo of the ghoul in the graveyard, down to the scowl. "Have someone see to that. Now."

She wants to point out that it is just a cut, that it hardly even hurts, that it's not her fault hands bleed so much, that one clumsy mistake hardly merits this much anger. Instead she just grabs her sketchpad and stomps up the grassy slope, through the garden and back into the house.

She was only trying to help.

His voice in your mouth,
telling me to come back,
to come back, to come home.

Chapter Ten

Olivia finds Edgar in the kitchen.

"Oh dear," he says, looking down at her hand, the kerchief gone rust-red where the cut bled through.

She shrugs, her stomach growling at the sight of the porridge pot on the stove, the contents long cooled to glue, but Edgar points her to the sink. She rinses the cut as he digs up a first aid box and lays out iodine and gauze. As he works, his hands are steady, his touch is light.

"I was in the army," he says casually, a safety pin between his teeth. "Had to patch up my share of battle wounds." He smiles, studying her hand. "But I think you'll live." He cleans the cut and binds it, winding a narrow white bandage around her palm and pinning it there. It feels like overkill for such a narrow cut, but he treats it with a surgeon's care. "Do try to keep your blood on the inside, though."

Something shudders in the doorway, and Olivia glances toward it, hoping to catch her mother's half-formed face. But it's yet another ghoul, this one younger, thinner, wasting, nothing but jutting ribs, a knee, a nose.

"Old houses," says Edgar, following her gaze. "Full of sounds you don't quite hear, and things you don't quite see."

She waits until he's finished with her hand and then asks, *Is Gallant haunted?* And even though she knows the answer is yes, she's surprised when Edgar nods.

"I'm sure it is," he says. "A house like this has too much history, and history always brings its share of ghosts. But it's not a bad thing," he adds, packing up his kit. "Ghosts were people once, and people come in all ways, good and bad and what's between. Sure, maybe some are out to frighten, but others, I think, are just watching, wishing they could help."

She looks back at the ghoul. It shrinks beneath her gaze, slipping back behind the doorframe.

As Edgar puts away the first aid kit, Olivia picks at the bandage on her hand.

Back at Merilance, someone was always getting scraped up, burning their fingers on the stove, or plucking gravel out of their knees. If you were lucky, the matrons would wave you off, say it was the cost of being clumsy. If you weren't, they'd douse it in rubbing alcohol, which hurt twice as much as any wound.

Sometimes a younger girl would cut herself and cry at the sight of blood. Sometimes an older one would pick her up and say, "It doesn't hurt," as if the words alone would make it true. An incantation, a spell to banish pain by denying its existence.

No one ever said them to Olivia—no one ever needed to—but she's lost count of the times she said them to herself.

When Agatha rapped her knuckles with a ruler.

It doesn't hurt.

When Clara pricked her with a sewing pin.

It doesn't hurt.

When Anabelle tore the pages from her mother's book.

"Does it hurt?" asks Edgar when he sees her fussing with the bandage.

The question catches her off guard, but Olivia shakes her head. He cuts a thick slice of bread and butters it and drops it in a skillet. The smell is heavenly, and she watches, mouth watering as he smears the toast with raspberry jam.

And sets it in front of her.

"There," he says, "that will put the life back in you."

Olivia takes a bite, melting a little with the sugar on her tongue.

He nods at her sketchpad. "What have you got there?"

Olivia licks the jam from her fingers and thumbs through the pages so he can see the last few drawings she's made, of the garden, and the orchard, and the wall.

"These are very good," he says, even though they're just beginnings, the pencil layered on itself, finding light and dark and line. "I remember, your mother always liked to draw."

Olivia frowns, thinking of the strange ink splotches in the journal. She wouldn't call those drawings. She takes another bite, the raspberries bursting brightly in her mouth. Edgar sees her smile as she chews.

"Hannah made the jam," he says. "Tom used to drizzle honey over—" He stops himself, startled, as if he tripped. A shadow crosses his face, there and then gone. "But the berries were so sweet last year, hardly needed any sugar."

Olivia lifts a hand to ask, but Edgar is already moving toward the door, saying something about a shutter that needs fixing, and she is left to add the name to the list in her head, along with all the other secrets Gallant seems to be keeping. The uncle who did not write her letter. Matthew's supposed curse. The colorless weeds in the garden. The wall that is not a wall. And this Tom no one wants to speak of. She conjures the field of Priors in her head, the short tombstones like spaced-out teeth, but she didn't see a Thomas there.

Olivia finishes her toast, tucks the sketchpad beneath her arm, and goes searching for the study. Moving through the halls, she's struck again by the size of this place, designed for forty instead of four. A skeleton staff, that's what it's called when there are so few left to manage a manor so large, but the residents of Gallant are less a skeleton than a handful of mismatched bones. And the house, the house is a maze, hall after hall and room after room, some grand and some small and most closed up, hills of furniture buried beneath crisp white sheets.

Beyond a pair of double doors she discovers a sprawling room, the kind designed for feasts or balls. Its floor is pale wood, inlaid with those same twisting circles. Its ceiling vaults high overhead, two stories, maybe three, and glass doors run along the far wall, a balcony beyond.

It is the grandest space she's ever seen, and she doesn't know what comes over her, but she twirls, bare feet whispering across the wood.

And then, at last, she finds the study.

She was beginning to think it was a trick of her mind, a dream, that she would search the entire house only to learn that no such room existed.

But here is the narrow hall, the waiting door.

Her fingers trail over the wallpaper, the way they did the night before, and the polished handle of the door gives way. There is no window, and she doesn't want to risk a lamp, so she leaves the door open, light spilling in from the hall. She pads forward, floorboards creaking softly underfoot until she reaches a thin dark rug that pools beneath the desk.

There on top is the strange metal sculpture, two houses set within concentric rings. Not just any house, but two small replicas of Gallant.

They perch on either side, facing each other at the center of the curving frame. Metal rings surround each house, and more surround the two together. Olivia cannot help herself. She lifts her fingertip to the outer ring, and gives it the slightest push, and the whole thing trips into motion.

She holds her breath, afraid that any second it will topple and clatter to the floor, but it's as if it were designed to move. The two houses turn like dancers, sliding away and then coming back to face each other. Each follows its own arc, each the center of its own small orbit. She watches, mesmerized, studying the steady revolution until it slows.

The houses move through their orbits one last time, and Olivia reaches out again to stop the motion as they come to face each other. She leans closer. It's strange, but from this angle, the rings between them look almost—almost—like a wall.

Olivia turns to a clean page in her sketchbook and draws the sculpture, trying to capture the sense of movement, the clean, almost mathematical lines of the device. She rounds the desk, to get another angle, and notices the drawer. It juts out like a bottom lip, a bit of paper caught in the corner. She tugs at the handle, and for a moment it sticks, then judders open.

Inside, a handful of loose paper, crisp and white, and a small black book. She peels it open and finds page after page of notes in a blocky hand. No, not notes. *Places.*

THE LARIMER SCHOOL
50 BELLWEATHER PLACE
BIRMINGHAM

HOLLINGWELL HOME
12 IDRIS ROW
MANCHESTER

FARRINGTON ORPHANAGE
5 FARRINGTON WAY
BRISTOL

Olivia turns past page after page, until she finds it, there, in the middle of the fourth.

MERILANCE SCHOOL FOR INDEPENDENT GIRLS
9 WINDSOR ROAD
NEWCASTLE

Footsteps sound in the hall.

Years of raiding matrons' rooms has trained her well, and in a moment the book is back and the drawer is shut and she is on the floor behind the grand old desk, tucked between the chair and the wood, heart fluttering even as her limbs go still.

She holds her breath and waits as the footsteps cross the threshold, as they cross from the bare wood onto the rug.

"How odd," says Hannah, "I could have sworn this door was shut."

Her voice is light and loud; she isn't talking to herself.

"You're not the first child to hide in this house," she says. "But most of them were playing games. Come on out now. I'm too old to get down on the floor."

Olivia sighs and rises to her feet. When Hannah reaches for

her, she retreats a step, on instinct, her bandaged palm tucked like a secret behind her back.

Hannah's hand falls, sadness dancing in her eyes.

"Goodness, girl, you're not in trouble. If you want to look around, have at it. After all, this is your house."

My house, thinks Olivia, the words tangling like hope inside her chest. Hannah's gaze drifts to the sculpture on the desk, and her mood seems to sour at the sight of it.

"Come on," she says, "it's getting late."

When the sun begins to set, they close the house up like a tomb.

Olivia follows Hannah from room to room, standing on chairs and stools to help pull the massive shutters in and slide the windows down. It seems such a waste, to shut themselves inside when the weather is so nice, but Hannah explains, "A place this wild, the outside is always trying to get in."

They eat in the kitchen, gathered round a table scraped and dented with wear. No lines of loud girls. No matrons perched like crows around the room. Just Hannah and Edgar, chatting easily as he pulls a tray from the oven, a towel over one shoulder, as she scoops vegetables into a bowl, as Olivia lays out four plates, even though Matthew isn't there, and it scares her, how good this feels. Like hot soup in winter, the warmth spreading with every sip.

"Here we are," says Edgar, depositing a tray of beef medallions on the table.

"What happened to your hand?" asks Hannah, catching sight of the bandage wrapped around her palm.

"Field injury," says Edgar. "Nothing I couldn't handle."

"You were a lucky find," she says, kissing his cheek. The gesture is so simple, so chaste, and yet, there are years of warmth behind it. Olivia feels her cheeks flush.

"Just goes to show," says Hannah, "I should put ads in the paper more often."

An ad in the paper? Olivia asks, catching Edgar's eye, but he only winks and rises.

"Put the right words into the world," he says, "never know what you'll catch."

Olivia stills.

I have sent these letters to every corner of the country.

May this be the one that finds you.

"Besides," says Edgar, taking his seat. "I thought our guest could use a proper meal."

Guest. The word cuts through her like a cold wind. She tries not to wince as Hannah passes a bowl of roast potatoes and parsnips, seasoned with salt. "Eat up."

It is a feast, and the day in the garden has left her famished. Olivia has never eaten so well. When she finally slows, Hannah asks about her life before the letter came. Olivia signs, and Edgar translates, and Hannah listens, one hand to her mouth as she explains how she was found on the steps of Merilance, how she has been there for nearly all her life.

Olivia does not tell them about the matrons, or the other girls, about the chalkboard or the garden shed or Anabelle. It is already beginning to feel like another life, a chapter in a book that she can simply close and leave. And she wants to. Because she wants to stay at Gallant. Even if Matthew does not want her there. She wants to stay and make this house a home. She wants to stay and learn its secrets, wants to know why they are so frightened of the dark, what happened to all the other Priors, what Matthew meant when he called this place cursed. But when she lifts her hands to ask, a shadow twitches in the doorway. She glances over, expecting a ghoul, but it's Matthew. He goes to the sink, scrubbing the garden from his hands.

He glances at Olivia. "Still here," he mutters, but Hannah only smiles and pats her bandaged hand.

"Nearest car's in the shop," she says. "Be a few days before it can come out."

Olivia can see the glimmer in the woman's eyes, a glint like mischief. Another lie. But Matthew only sighs and sets the soap aside.

"Sit and eat," urges Edgar, but her cousin shakes his head, murmurs about not being hungry, even though his too-thin body is begging for a meal. He leaves, taking the air out of the room as he goes. Hannah and Edgar pick at their food, each trying to fill the space with easy talk, but it comes out stiff, awkward.

Olivia catches Edgar's eye. *Is he sick?*

He flashes Hannah a look and then says, "Matthew's tired.

Tired can be a kind of sick, if it lasts long enough."

He's telling the truth, some version of it, but a draft runs through the words. There is so much they are not saying. It hangs in the air, and Olivia wishes they could go back to before Matthew came in. But their plates are empty now, and Hannah gets to her feet, saying she'll make him a tray, if Edgar will take it up. And Edgar sees Olivia staring at him, hands raised to ask about Matthew and the house, but he stands and turns his back. She hates that he can do that, that all he has to do to silence her is look away.

She stifles a yawn, even though it's not yet nine, and Hannah offers her a shortbread biscuit and tells her a hot bath and a warm bed will do her well before shooing her from the kitchen.

She takes the long way to the stairs, past the narrow foyer and the garden door. It must be a cloudy night. No moonlight streams in through the little window, but the hall isn't empty. Her uncle's ghoul stands like a watchman, its back to her and its eyes on the dark.

The master of the house is hungry.

He is worn thin with it, that hunger. It gnaws, like teeth on bone, until he cannot stand the ache. Until his fingers flex, stiff in their joints. It is unyielding. This place is unyielding.

He walks through the ruined garden.

Past the empty fountain and across the barren grounds, through the brittle land that rolls away from the house like a bolt of cloth left to rot in the cupboard. Moth-eaten. Threadbare.

The fruit is rotten. The ground is parched. The house is falling like sand through the glass. He has eaten every morsel, every scrap, and nothing is left. He is feasting on himself, now. Wasting a little more with every passing night.

He is a fire running out of air. But it is not over yet. He will burn, and burn, and burn until the house crumbles, until the world gives way.

All he needs is a breath.

All he needs is a drop.

All he needs is her.

And so he sits back in his throne and closes his eyes and dreams.

Part Three
THINGS UNSAID

Chapter Eleven

Olivia is so tired, and yet, again, she cannot sleep.

Her limbs sink into the bed, heavy from the fresh air and the garden's work, but her mind is tangled up in questions. She tosses and turns, feeling the hours tick past as she watches the candle drip and gutter on her bedside table, and she is about to give up and throw the covers off when she hears it.

The subtle creak of the door drifting open.

Even though she turned the lock.

Olivia holds her breath as bare feet whisper on the wood behind her, and then, a body lowers itself onto the other side of the bed, the mattress denting with the weight. Slowly, she wills herself to turn over, sure that it is only a trick of her tired mind, sure that the room will be empty and she will see—

A young woman sits on the edge of the bed.

She is older than Olivia, but not by much, her skin sun kissed, ribbons of brown hair spilling down her back. When she turns her head, candlelight dances across her high cheek, her narrow chin, tracing the angles and lines from the portrait that morning. The ones pressed here and there into Olivia's own face.

Her mother looks over her shoulder. A smile flickers across her face, all mischief. And in that moment she is young, a girl. But then the candle shifts, and the shadows cut the other way, and she is a woman again.

Her fingers slide over the sheets, and Olivia doesn't know whether to reach for her mother's hand or retreat, and in the end, she does neither, because she cannot move. Her limbs are leaden in the bed, and perhaps she should be afraid, but she isn't. She cannot take her eyes from Grace Prior, not as she climbs onto the bed, not as she lowers herself beside Olivia, not as she curls herself in like a mirror, reflecting the angles of her daughter's limbs, the bend of her neck, the incline of her head, as if it were a game.

Her bare feet are stained with dirt, the same way Olivia's were before she soaked away the soil, as if she's been running in the garden. But her mother's hands are delicate and clean, as her fingers graze the air over the bandage around Olivia's palm, worry flitting across her face. Her hand drifts up to Olivia's cheek.

The touch, when it lands, is warm, the gesture gentle. The candlelight doesn't reach the sliver of space between their bodies, and her mother's face is dark, unreadable. But Olivia can see the shine of her teeth when she smiles and leans in and speaks.

Her voice is soft, familiar, not high and sweet, but low and soothing.

The faintest rasp, like gravel, in her throat.

"*Olivia, Olivia, Olivia,*" says her mother, as if it's an incantation, the last words of a spell, and maybe it is, because just like that, she wakes up.

There is a dead thing in her bed.

The candle has gone out. The room is pitch black, and yet Olivia can see the ghoulish figure, nestled there, the way her mother was, one rotting hand still lifted to her cheek.

Olivia's limbs have come unstuck, and she recoils, scrambling back, not realizing how close she is to the edge of the bed until it disappears beneath her and she tumbles off the side, landing hard on the wooden floor. The pain is enough to clear her head, and she surges to her feet.

But the ghoul is already gone.

Olivia lets out a shaky breath and lifts her good palm to her cheek, holding in her mother's touch.

But that part only happened in the dream. The things she sees cannot touch her. They are not really there.

She paws through the dark, finds a box of matches and a fresh taper. Light strikes and blooms, shadows dancing as she takes up her sketchpad and pencil and begins to draw. Not the ghoul of Grace Prior, but the woman she was in the dream. Quick, rough lines, the pencil hissing as she tries to capture not so much her mother's face but the softness of her touch, the sadness in her eyes, the way she said her name. *Olivia, Olivia, Olivia.* Her pencil scratches across the paper, racing ahead of the fog, the forgetting.

She's halfway through the sketch when someone screams.

The pencil skips, the tip breaking as Olivia twists toward the noise.

She has heard screams before. The shrill shout of children playing games. The injured howl following a broken arm. The terrified yelp of a girl waking to find insects in her bed.

This scream is different.

It is keening.

It is shuddering breath.

It is a strained and desperate sob, and Olivia is already on her feet, hurrying toward her bedroom door, trying to pull it open. She panics for an instant when it holds, before remembering the small gold key. It turns with a click, and Olivia plunges out into the hall, half expecting the screams to halt the moment she crosses the threshold.

But they keep going.

A door hangs open down the hall, the pool of light on the floor filled with moving shadows, and she can hear Hannah and Edgar now, the struggle of bodies, and she realizes who is screaming the same instant she reaches the door and sees Matthew thrashing in the bed.

The screams resolve into words, into pleas. *"I can't leave him. I can't leave him. WHY WON'T YOU LET ME HELP HIM?"*

His eyes are open, but he is somewhere else. He doesn't see

Hannah, whispering urgently, her hair wild, doesn't see Edgar as he fights to hold him down, doesn't see Olivia standing wide-eyed in the doorway.

"It is just a dream," soothes Hannah. "It's just a dream. It cannot hurt you."

Her mother's promise pouring out of Hannah's mouth, but the words aren't true.

He is clearly hurting.

A wretched sob escapes his throat, and it is unnerving, to see her cousin like this, split open, the vivid red of him laid bare. He looks so young, so scared, and Olivia tears her gaze away from the bed to the rest of the room. To the tray of food he barely touched, to the shutters latched tight beyond the glass, to a sharp-edged shape against the far wall, a sheet cast over it.

A cry wrenches her back to the bed. Hannah and Edgar are trying to force Matthew's hands into a pair of leather straps. Panic ripples through her, and she has to stifle the urge to rush forward, to pull them away. It shocks her, the force of that feeling, and she manages one step before Edgar's eyes knife toward her, and she sees the pain in them, the grief that stops her cold.

Matthew strains and pleads as the loops pull tight around his wrists, and then falls feverishly back against the bed, chest heaving. Thin lines of salt slide down his cheeks and into his hair. She doesn't know if they are sweat or tears.

"Please," he murmurs, voice cracking. "They're hurting him."

That word, a barb at the edge of his voice. Not *me*, but *him*.

"No," says Hannah, pressing him down. "They cannot hurt him anymore."

She tips a cloudy glass of liquid to Matthew's lips, and soon his pleading fades to pained murmurs. "He's resting now," she says, exhaustion brimming in her throat. "You must rest, too."

Olivia didn't see Edgar pull away from the bed. Didn't see him come toward the door. Toward her. Not until he is right there, blocking her view of the room.

Go back to bed, he signs, his face tired.

What is wrong with him? she asks.

But Edgar only shakes his head. *Bad dreams,* he says.

And then he closes the door.

Olivia lingers in the darkened hall, between two streams of light—the one pouring through her open door, and the thin strand beneath Matthew's. And when she finally retreats back to her own room, her own bed, the unfinished sketch lying faceup on the crumpled covers, she runs her fingers over the graphite and thinks of dreams. The kind that reach through the folds of sleep and into your bed. The kind that can caress your cheek or drag you down into the dark.

There is no rest in sleep.
These dreams will be the death of me.

Chapter Twelve

The next morning, there is blood on her sheets.

Olivia flinches at the sight, wondering if it's her time, but the stains are less dots or streaks and more fingers dug into the bedding. Sure enough, the bandage on her palm has come loose, the cut opened in her sleep, a restless night played out in handprints.

She goes to the bathroom sink, brushing the dried blood from her hands as if it were dust. She rinses her palm, waits to see if it will bleed again, but it doesn't. She runs a thumb over the narrow line, the scab like a raised red thread, a vine, a root. She decides to let it air as she searches her mother's closet, pulls out a dress the soft, dark green of summer leaves. It skims her knees, and when she turns, the skirt flares out like petals.

Her sketchpad lies abandoned in the sheets. Her mother's half-formed face stares up from the paper, the other half, where the candlelight could not reach, rendered as a streak of shadow. Olivia closes the pad and tucks it under her arm.

As she steps into the hall, her eyes go straight to Matthew's door. She creeps forward, pressing her ear to the wood, and hears—nothing. Not the unsettling sobs or the ragged breath, not even the rasp and rustle of sheets. Her fingers drift to the knob, but the memory of his pain forces her back, and she turns, heading instead for the stairs.

Below, the house is quiet.

Perhaps everyone is still asleep. Olivia looks around and realizes she has no idea what time it is. Back at Merilance, there were bells, whistles, sharp sounds to mark the passing hours, to summon the girls to and from their beds, to usher them from prayers to class to chores and back again. Here, the only time that seems to matter is the passing of the sun, the moment when day becomes night.

But the house has roused itself. The shutters have been thrown, sunlight spilling through the foyer and down the halls, catching dust motes in the air.

Someone cries out, and she jumps, only to realize the sound isn't human, but the high-pitched whistle of a kettle. By the time she reaches the kitchen, it is singing, alone on the stove. Olivia turns the burner off.

"Well, you're up early."

She turns and finds Hannah mounting the cellar stairs, a bag of flour in one arm. Her brown curls are wrangled back, a smile creasing the corners of her mouth, but her eyes are tired.

"Oh to be young again," she says, setting the flour down hard enough to send up a small white cloud. "And need so little sleep." She nods at the kettle. "You do the tea, I'll do the toast."

Olivia lifts the kettle, careful to avoid the cut on her palm. She scalds the pot, and ladles in a spoonful of loose tea as Hannah slices bread, and for a few moments they move like cogs in the same clock, like the houses in the study sculpture, circling each other in an easy arc. As the tea steeps and the bread toasts, she opens the sketchpad, paging back past the drawing of her mother to the image of the strange metal globe.

She turns the paper toward Hannah and taps the page, the question clear.

What is this?

For a second, the only sound is the knife scraping butter over toast. But it is a heavy kind of silence, the one people use when they know the answer to something but can't decide if they should tell it. "Old houses are full of old things," she says at last. "Matthew might know." Olivia rolls her eyes—so far her cousin has been no help at all.

"Fine day," adds Hannah, sliding two plates of jam-and-buttered toast across the counter. "Too fine to be inside. Take this one out to Edgar, would you? He's somewhere in the yard."

Olivia sighs at the dismissal.

It takes both hands and all of her focus to get one cup of tea, two plates of toast, and the sketchpad out into the garden without spilling or breaking or losing anything. But Hannah is right; it is a fine day. A shine of dew lingers on the grass beneath her feet, but the mist and chill are burning off, and the sky overhead is a milky blue.

She finds Edgar up on a ladder, mending one of the shutters. He waves good morning, nods for her to set the toast on the ground. Olivia hesitates, worried that something might get at it there, a bird or a mouse. Only, now that she thinks of it, she hasn't seen any animals.

It's strange, really, on all this land. She doesn't know much about the countryside, of course, but she saw cows and sheep on the drive up, and she imagines a dozen smaller things, rabbits, sparrows, moles, might take up residence on the estate.

Even at Merilance they found the occasional mouse, and the sky was always full of gulls. If Gallant were a storybook, there would surely be a dog by the hearth or a cat sunning on the drive, a flock of magpies in the orchard, or a crow on the wall. But there's nothing. Only an airy silence.

She carries her breakfast to the stone bench and flops down on it.

According to Matron Agatha, proper girls sit with their knees together and their ankles crossed. Olivia sits cross-legged, knees falling open and green skirt fanning across her lap as she eats.

The sun catches the metal rim of a bucket nearby, a pair of gloves draped over the edge, but the cut on her palm is still fresh, so she leaves it, decides to draw the house instead.

She turns to a blank page, begins to draw, and soon Gallant takes shape beneath her hand, growing from a few quick strokes into a thing with walls and windows, chimneys and steepled roofs. Here are the wings and the ballroom balcony and the garden door. Here is the bay window, the only one that has no shutters, and here is the dark shape of the piano beyond.

She is just adding Edgar on his ladder, little more than a thin shadow cast against the massive house, when she hears footsteps coming through the garden.

Movement is a kind of voice. She can tell a person from the way they walk. Edgar shuffles slightly, one leg stiffer than the other. Hannah's steps are steady and short and surprisingly quiet. Matthew's stride is long but weighted, as if his boots are too big or too heavy.

She hears her cousin trudging down the path and looks up to find him pulling on his garden gloves. She waits for him to cut a look her way, to comment on the fact that she is still here, but he says nothing, only kneels and begins to tend the roses. There can't be more weeds so soon, and yet there are, gray strands coming free with every tug.

His sleeves are rolled up, and she can see the bruises blooming where the gloves end at his wrists, and he looks so thin she fears that if the sun hits him just right, she might be able to see through, so she nudges the rest of her toast toward him. The plate scrapes, china on stone, and his eyes flick up.

"I'm fine," he says in a hollow, automatic way, even though he looks worse than most of the ghouls, so she pushes the plate again, eliciting another awful scratch, and he scowls at her, annoyed, and she scowls back, and a moment later he tugs off one glove and takes the toast. He doesn't say thank you.

She returns to drawing Gallant, but she cannot shake the sense she's being watched, can feel the weight of eyes against her back. She glances over at Matthew, but his head is down, his attention on his work. She looks over her shoulder, but all she sees is the wall.

Olivia twists round and turns back to her sketchpad, flipping through until she finds the abandoned drawing. She looks from the paper to the wall, trying to find the place where she went wrong, is still tapping her pencil against the page when Matthew's shadow falls across the paper.

He glances down at the sketchpad, his expression souring at the sight of the wall. She holds her breath, waiting for him to speak, and when he doesn't, she turns to a blank page, and writes.

What happened to your father?

But when she holds up the paper, Matthew's eyes barely land on it before he looks away. She shoves it back in front of him, forcing him to read, but his eyes refuse to settle on the words. "Wasting your time," he mutters, and at last she understands. It's not that he doesn't want to read, it's that he *can't.*

He sees the understanding on her face and scowls.

"I'm not stupid," he snaps. Olivia shakes her head. She knows too well what's it like when people take one weakness and define you by it. "I just—I never got the hang of it. The letters won't sit still. The words get jumbled up."

She nods, and then begins again, pencil scratching across the page.

"I told you—" he growls, but she holds up her index finger, a silent order to wait as she sketches as quickly as she can. The man takes shape on the paper, not as he was, half-formed at the garden door, but as he was in the portrait hall. Arthur Prior. She turns the sketch toward her cousin, and she might as well have slammed a door in his face.

"He died," he says. "It doesn't matter how."

Matthew fixes his gaze ahead, past the garden, to the wall.

Olivia turns the page, pencil hovering. She's still trying to put her other questions into pictures when he says, "There must always be a Prior at the gate."

His voice is low and brims with bitterness, but the words spill out like something memorized.

"Always. That's what my father said. As if we've always been at Gallant. But we haven't. The Priors didn't build this house. Gallant was already here. It called out to our family, and like fools, we came."

Olivia frowns, confused. The *house* did not write her that letter. Someone in it did. Someone who wanted her to come. Someone who claimed to be her uncle.

"We came to Gallant once, and now we cannot leave. We are bound here, chained to the house and the wall and the thing beyond, and it will not end until there are no Priors left."

My father said I was the last.

"Have you begun to hear it yet?" He looks at her, eyes fever bright. "Does it come into your dreams?"

Olivia shakes her head, uncertain what he means. She has dreamed twice, and both times were of her mother. But Matthew's voice rings through her, the harsh sob she heard the night before.

"You don't know what it feels like," he says, pain breaking like a tide across his face. "What it can do. What it can take."

What is this *it* he speaks of? She reaches for his hand, but Matthew is already moving away, the last thing he says little more than a murmur.

"If it hasn't found you yet, there is still time."

And then he is gone, marching up the path, no doubt searching for Hannah to ask about the car. Olivia presses her hands to her temples, a headache forming there. Matthew's words are like her mother's, another needless riddle. Why can't her family speak in simple truths? She looks down at the drawing.

. . . chained to the house and the wall and the thing beyond . . .

Her gaze drifts up, past the garden. Her cousin clearly is not well. He doesn't eat, he cannot sleep, he talks of curses, of gates, but there's just a battered stretch of rock at the edge of the garden. Olivia stands and scans the grounds. There's no sign of Matthew now. Or Edgar, though his ladder still leans against the house.

She doesn't make a straight line for the wall. She just . . . drifts toward it. Through the garden, past the last line of roses, down the gentle slope of grass.

The old ghoul in the graveyard watches her go. It doesn't

abandon the orchard, but she can see the tilt of its half-there head, its arms folded across its missing chest, clearly displeased to see her at the wall. *I know, I know,* she thinks. But she doesn't stop.

As Olivia nears the wall, she sees why her drawings never worked. It's the light. The sun doesn't seem to hit the wall, not as it should. Even though it is behind her now, casting her shadow down the hill. Even though it should shine directly on the stones, it doesn't reach. Instead, the shadows bend and pool around the wall, and Olivia shivers a little as she steps into that strange cool shade.

And then, at last, she sees the door.

She can't believe she didn't notice it before. It's old iron, a shade darker than the surrounding stone, and if the sun had fallen on it, perhaps she would have seen it sooner. Still, now that she has seen it, she cannot imagine thinking the wall was solid stone.

The gate, she thinks, reaching out to touch the door, shocked to feel how cold the metal is. There's a small handle, sculpted like an ivy runner, but when she tries it, it's locked. She crouches, looking for a keyhole, but there's none.

How strange.

What good is a locked door in a wall that simply ends? The wall isn't even very long—a dozen paces to either side and she would reach the crumbled edge. Her feet are already carrying her toward it when something makes her slow, then stop.

According to Matthew, there is something *beyond* the wall.

Olivia chews her lip. It is ridiculous, of course. She can see the space beyond, the open field stretching out to either side. But she cannot bring herself to round it. Instead, she returns to the door.

There is a narrow gap where the iron gate meets the wall, the width of her finger, the space interrupted by a pair of bolts, and the sight of it tickles something in her mind, but she cannot place it. She rises on her toes, pressing her eye to the gap.

She has read enough stories about doorways, thresholds, and for a moment she imagines herself balanced at the edge of something grand, something dark or dangerous—but when she looks, all she sees is a field of tallgrass, swaying in the breeze, the craggy mountains in the distance.

Her heart sinks a little, and she pulls back, feeling silly.

Of course, the wall is just a wall. Nothing more.

Something cracks, and to her right a few bits of stone tumble free, the sound like rain on an old tin roof. It's one of the spots Matthew tried to patch—she can tell by the color, lighter than the surrounding rock—but the mortar is brittle, already flaking, traces of it shed onto the grass, as if the wall had stirred and shaken off the mends like dust. Up close, she sees the source of the latest crack: a thin gray weed has forced its way through. She reaches out to pull it before remembering the cut along her palm and Matthew's fury. Instead, she takes up a fallen stone and wedges it back in place.

"Olivia!"

Her name rings out, drawn thin across the yard, and when she looks back, one hand to her eyes to shield the sun, she sees Edgar waving, the ladder leaning on one shoulder.

"Give me a hand?" he calls, and Olivia jogs toward him, out of the cold shadow and into the sun, the warmth shocking but welcome. As she crosses the grassy rise, she hears the soft scrape of more stones coming free.

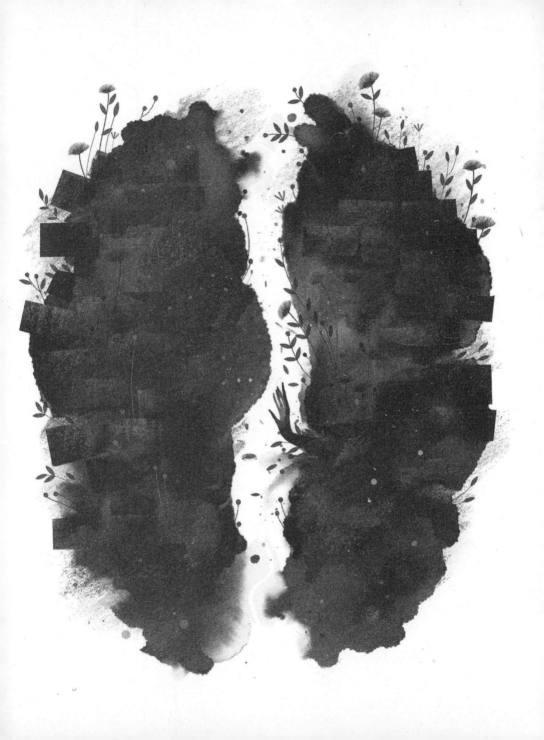

Chapter Thirteen

The candle dips and gutters but doesn't go out.

It's late, but Olivia sits, wide awake, in the center of her bed. She turns through her mother's journal, hoping for answers, but finds only the same entries, so long memorized, and maddeningly vague.

There is no rest
slept in your ashes
When you came apart
want to fall asleep but he always finds me there

Her mother and her cousin, both haunted by their dreams. Did Grace wither, like Matthew? Did the skin beneath her eyes bruise and her face go thin? Was it madness, or sickness, or was she simply so tired that they became the same? And if it happened to them, will it happen to her?

It hasn't found you yet …

Olivia turns from the journal to her sketchpad, the drawings she made of Matthew and the house and the garden wall. She feels as though she's standing at the center of a maze, each turn a question she cannot scale, each break leading her deeper into the tangled dark.

She keeps one ear tuned, braced for the sound of Matthew's screams, but the hall is quiet, the shadows in her own room empty. The only sounds are the soft whisper of the candle burning and the brittle creak of the pages turning.

Olivia presses her palms against her eyes, frustration welling with the urge to slam a door or break a pot in a garden shed, something to drag the feelings out, give them shape and sound. Instead, she shoves the books away and slumps back against the pillows.

A second later, she hears the telltale crack of a pencil hitting the floor, then rolling beneath the bed.

Leave it, she thinks, but she has the strangest feeling that if she does, the house will snatch it up, swallow it down into the cracks between the wooden boards, the gaps between the floors, and it is her favorite pencil. She sighs, throwing the covers off, and gets up, crouching to look beneath the bed.

She braces herself for a rotting face, the grizzly gossamer of dirt-stained hair, a broken smile. The ghoul in the dorm used to lie like that, beneath the cots, chin resting on its folded arms in the dark, as if anyone but Olivia would see it there.

But there is no ghoul beneath the bed. Only dust and darkness and the faint outline of her pencil, just out of reach. As Olivia lies flat and stretches forward to grab hold, she sees something else. A solid shadow, wedged like a secret between the head-board and the wall, its bottom corner sticking down.

It's a book.

She cannot tell if it simply fell behind the bed and got stuck, or if it was hidden there on purpose, but when she tucks the pencil behind her ear and pulls at the shape, it comes free. Her heart lurches at the feel of it—thin and soft. Not a book at all.

A *journal*.

Olivia shimmies backward into the pool of candlelight on the bedroom floor and sits there, studying the cover. A gilded *G* curves across the front, and she stares, perplexed. It is her mother's journal. Only it's not, because when Olivia stands, she sees her mother's journal, the one she's always had, sitting among the tangled sheets where she left it. Besides, her mother's journal is green and worn with age, dented by those two strange lines, pages sticking too far out where they were torn and put back. This one is soft, and clean, and far less abused.

And it's red. Just like the one in her dream.

She runs her thumb over the gilded G, hardly worn, imagines her mother being given not one, but two. A set. She holds her breath as she peels back the cover, the air rushing out when she sees the words, the handwriting soft and full of curls, the way it was in the first pages of her journal, before the hand lost its steady grip, before the entries grew strange and broken and blotted out.

Olivia spent years poring over the riddle of her mother's book, scrutinizing every line for clues. Now she turns through page after page, marveling at the wealth of new words.

Arthur is in such a mood today.

She flips past, finds Hannah's name.

Hannah said that if I ruin one more dress, she'll make me wear trousers. I told her that would be fine, so long as I could have a pair of boots to match.

Several pages later, she finds Edgar.

Something let the bird out of its cage, and now I cannot find it. Arthur says it's lost now, and Edgar says it's for the best, that birds like sky more than windowsills. I left the window open, hoping it would come back, and Father nearly had my head.

How strange, to see the doors flung open onto another life. There is no mysterious "you" in these entries, no mention of moving shadows or bones with stories like marrow or voices in the dark. There *are* drawings, here and there, sketches of a birdcage, a rose, a pair of hands, but they are small and precise, folded in along the margins of the words, so unlike the wild, amorphous inks in the other book.

Olivia skims a dozen mundane entries—musings on how Arthur is driving Grace mad, on her mother's absence, her father's worsening cough. On Hannah and Edgar and the fact no one seems to notice they're falling in love—before she snags on one.

Last night I went beyond the wall.

Olivia's breath catches in her throat, her eyes already rushing on.

I wanted to see it for myself. I wanted to know if it was real, or if I'm expected to grow and wither here for nothing more than superstition. Wouldn't that be funny? If it were just a story, passed from one Prior to the next until all of us forgot that it was fiction? All of us, given to the same mad delusion?

That big wide world, and us just sitting here, staring at a wall.

Father calls it a prison, and we the keepers, but that is a lie. We are as much prisoners here. Bound to these grounds, this house, that garden.

Olivia stops, Matthew's voice echoing through her head. *We came to Gallant once, and now we cannot leave. We are bound here.* She pushes him out of her thoughts and reads on.

Arthur says that death waits beyond the wall. But the truth is, death is everywhere. Death comes for the roses and the apples, it comes for the mice and the birds. It comes for us all. Why should death stop us from living?

So, I did it.

I went beyond the wall.

I shouldn't have. I thought—but it doesn't matter what I thought. Of course I'm not the first. Of course the stories are not fictions. I am not sorry. I'm not—But I understand now.

I will never go back.

Olivia's heart quickens as she turns the page.

No one ever needs to know.

I should not even write it here, but some part of me knows that if I don't, I'll begin to doubt myself. I'll think it was a dream. But you can't dream words onto paper. So here. Last night, I went beyond the wall.

And I met Death.

The words scrawl like weeds across the page. Olivia traces her fingers over them, half expecting them to twitch beneath her touch. Ink has dripped onto the paper, as if the writer's pen hovered, uncertain, before taking up again.

Not met, but saw, and that was close enough. With his four shadows and his dozen shades, all silent in the bones of the ruined house. It sounds like madness written down. It felt like madness when I witnessed it. A mad world, a fever dream.

Arthur caught me after, in the garden, shook me hard and asked if I'd been seen, and I said no.

I did not tell my brother how the tallest shadow found me in the hall, peeled away from his master like a long summer day. I did not tell my brother how he looked straight at me with those near-black eyes and pointed to the closest door, to the garden and the wall, head cocked. I did not tell my brother that the shadow let me go.

The entry ends. Olivia's hands are already turning the page. The next entry begins:

I wrote to him last night.

I went back, expected to find it gone, stolen like everything else that falls through the cracks, but it was still there, tucked between the iron and the stone, and I could tell by the angle it had been moved, and when I checked, I found that he had written back.

Another page, another entry.

I have lived at Gallant all my life. But home is meant to be a choice. I did not choose this house. I am tired of being bound to it.

Olivia turns, hoping for more, but the next page is torn, and the next, and the next, the following entries all ripped out, leaving only a few black beginnings near the binding, the inky curl of letters broken, words ripped in two. A breadcrumb trail of half-formed words.

> *Not comi—*
> *a prisone—*
> *togeth—*
> *we can f—*
> *tonigh—*

Olivia lets out a frustrated breath and turns back to the beginning.

Her mother went beyond the wall. She saw death, and four shadows, and a dozen shades. The tallest shadow helped her home. It is the stuff of fairy tales. Or something darker. A girl losing her mind? And yet, she was well enough to know how it sounded written down. And hasn't Olivia herself seen shades? The half-there girls back at Merilance. Her own mother and uncle trailing her through the halls of Gallant. Did Grace Prior see ghouls, too?

But what is the difference between a shadow and a shade?

Is it a riddle or a code?

She closes her eyes, trying to assemble the pieces, but her mind is too tired to find the edges, and nothing seems to fit, and eventually she blows out the candle with an exasperated breath and falls back into the bed.

And in the dark, she dreams.

Perhaps you are haunting me.
What a comforting thought.
Maybe it's you in the darkness.
I swear I've seen it move.

Chapter Fourteen

There is a man in the garden.

He stumbles, as if sick or drunk, falls down, and gets back to his feet, dragging his tired body past the flowers, pale in moonlight, past the trellises and hedges, past Olivia, who sits watching on the low stone bench, unable to move. He surges by, legs unsteady as he passes the final row of roses, and heads for the sloping stretch of grass toward the garden wall.

"You cannot have me!" he shouts, words shattering the quiet night. His voice is hoarse, exhausted. "You will not win."

He glances back over his shoulder, at the house, at her, and the light cuts across his haunted gaze, his hollowed cheeks. His face is half in shadow, but she recognizes that jaw, those deep-set eyes, the echo of Matthew's, but older. Her uncle. Arthur.

She watches, helpless, as he stumbles again, but this time he doesn't get back up. He sinks to his knees in the grass. An object glints in his hand, and at first she thinks it is a spade, but then the moonlight strikes the barrel. It is a gun.

"You say that you can make the nightmares stop." He looks up at the wall, eyes glassy in the dark. "Well, so can I."

The gun swings up against his temple.

Olivia wakes with the bang.

The sound rings through the room, and she is already up, racing barefoot toward the door. *It was just a dream,* she tells herself, but it felt so real. It was just a dream, but her dreams seem to reach into the waking world, and the gunshot is still echoing in her ears as she rushes into the hall. Matthew's door hangs open, lamplight pooling on the wooden floor, but there are no sobs, no signs of Hannah or Edgar wrestling him back onto the bed.

That bed is empty now, the sheets thrown back, the leather straps hanging to the floor.

Dread rolls through her. It was just a dream, but Matthew is not here, and she is certain that if she looks out into the garden, she will see a body slumped in the grass. Her window faces the front and the fountain. Matthew's room is across the hall, so it must look onto the garden and the wall. But when she goes to the window, the shutters are not just latched—they're locked.

Olivia hurries back down the hall, is halfway down the stairs when she hears it. Not a scream, or a shot, but a soft sequence of notes, rising and falling in scale.

Someone is playing the piano.

The melody wafts like smoke, thin and wispy, and Olivia's heart struggles to slow as she follows the sound down the stairs and through the maze of halls to the music room, the light spilling from the open door, and there is the glossy black shell of the piano, and Matthew, head bowed over the keys.

At first glance she almost mistakes him for a ghoul, hunched forward so far he looks nearly headless. But a ghoul wouldn't be able to touch the keys, let alone coax such music forth, and when he shifts, the lamplight falls on firm but narrow shoulders, limns the edges of his hair. He is solid enough.

Her gaze goes past him then, to the bay window, the moonlit garden sprawling beyond the glass. She searches the darkened lawn, but there is no body. Of course there is no body. It was just a dream.

Olivia shifts in the doorway, and the movement draws Matthew's notice.

He glances up, meeting her gaze in the glass. For a moment, his hands stop, the melody suspended, and she holds his gaze, waits for the annoyance to flash across his reflection. But there is no anger in his shoulders, no frustration in his jaw. Only weariness. He looks back down and starts again.

"Couldn't sleep," he says, and her eyes go to the bruises around his wrists. She knows his dreams are just as vivid as her own, images that taste and feel and sound like truth. Three nights in this house, and already she feels rattled. Judging by the cast of Matthew's skin, the hollows beneath his eyes, he has dealt with them far longer, and the dreams have been far worse.

There is no rest in sleep. These dreams will be the death of me.

"Don't hover," he says, but there's an invitation in the words, to come in or to go. Olivia drifts forward.

There are only two seats in the room, the bay window and the piano bench, and she cannot bring herself to sit in the window with her back to the garden, so she sits on the edge of the bench, watching his fingers drift over the keys, hands moving with the ease of practice. The song that wafts through the room is soft and winding and lonely. She knows that isn't the right word, but it is the only one that fits. The notes are lovely, but they make her feel like she is back in the garden shed.

"Do you play?"

Olivia shakes her head no, wonders if he can see the sadness in her face, or the hungry way she looks at the keys. But Matthew isn't looking at her. He isn't looking down either. Instead, he keeps his gaze on the window, on the night, on the moon-soaked garden and the distant wall, its edges traced with silver light.

He takes a long, slow breath and says, "My father showed me, when I was young."

He softens, a ghost of a smile crosses his face, and she does not recognize this Matthew.

He was a kind boy once.

His hands are so gentle on the keys. "My mother loved to hear him play. I wanted to learn, too, but he didn't know how to teach, couldn't remember how he had learned himself, so he sat me down one day and nodded at the keys and said, 'Watch and listen and figure it out.'"

Matthew's left hand never stops, but his right drifts to the keys right in front of her, plucking out three notes and looping them, over and over.

"Like this," he says. He withdraws again, and Olivia brings her own hand to the keys.

Something moves behind them, but Matthew doesn't seem to notice. Olivia looks up at the window, and in the reflection, glimpses the ghoul of an old woman, leaning in the shadow by the door, its face tilted as it listens.

"Go on," urges Matthew, and she begins to play. She knows it's not *playing* so much as making a circle of sound, but it's something, it's a start, and she feels herself smiling, caught up in the melody.

"My brother Thomas never got the hang of it," he says, and Olivia fumbles at the mention of that name. "He couldn't sit still long enough to learn. But I never thought of it as *still*. It's . . . something in you goes quiet, to make room for the song. These days, it feels like the closest thing I ever find to rest."

Olivia holds her breath, waiting for him to go on, to tell her what happened to Thomas, to explain why he is alone in this too-big house, why he cannot leave, though her mother did, why he spends his nights lashed to a bed, crying out for help.

But he doesn't say more. The moment passes.

Tomorrow she will find a way to ask these questions, tomorrow she will make him answer, but tonight she lets Matthew play in peace. Tonight the ghoul slips out of the room, and Olivia closes her eyes and lets the melody curl around her, her mind going quiet, to make room for the song. The darkest part of the night passes and thins. Together they keep the music going until dawn.

Chapter Fifteen

For the first time in years, Olivia sleeps late.

She barely remembers returning to her room or climbing back beneath the sheets. She knows only that it was already morning, pale light spilling in through the fog-laced garden and onto the piano as Matthew played. But when she reached her room, the shutters were still drawn, the room still dark, and sleep crashed over her, dragging her down not into dreams, but into sweet, familiar nothing.

When she surfaces again, it's to the white noise of heavy rain.

Hannah has come through—a pot of tea sits on the ottoman, but there's no steam, the contents long cold. The shutters are open, but the light outside is a waterlogged gray. The kind of gray that belongs to another world, another life. Her stomach tightens at the sight of it, the memory of gravel hissing beneath her shoes, abandoned flower beds and collapsing sheds and buildings like dull teeth.

Olivia swallows and listens to the storm, some small part of her afraid that Gallant has been nothing but a dream, that she is about to wake and find herself back at Merilance, crouching in the garden shed while rain drums its fingers on the old tin roof.

But then she hears Edgar's voice on the stairs, calling down to Hannah, and the fear unwinds. She is still here. It is still real.

And yet, just to be safe, Olivia searches her mother's wardrobe, dresses in the brightest thing she can find, as if the vivid blue of the dress is a defiance, a color that would never be found at Merilance. She is finishing the buttons when she hears it, beyond the window.

It's low, half-hidden by the steady curtain of rain, but she catches the rasp of tires on gravel, the rumble of an engine.

A *car*.

Panic lurches through her, and for a brief and terrifying second, she is sure that it has come for her. That she will look out the window and see the same black car that drove her away from Merilance, waiting like a hearse to take her back again. But when she brings herself to look past the fogging glass, down at the fountain and the drive, she sees Edgar jogging out to greet a butcher's truck, the trade of crates, a wave, and the man is back behind the wheel and pulling away.

Her fluttering pulse begins to settle. Her fingers relax where they were gripping the desk. She retreats, returning to the bed to collect her mother's journals. She finds the sketchpad among the tangled sheets, tucks all three beneath her arm and heads downstairs.

It is a wretched day outside, but inside, it's rather pleasant.

There is a sleepy air to everything. Wind whistles faintly against the house, rattling the open shutters, and with the sun buried behind so many clouds, it's hard to tell what time it is. It could be ten in the morning or six at night or anywhere between. Edgar is humming softly in the kitchen, but the low crackle of wood draws her toward the sitting room, where she finds Hannah tucked in a chair, feet propped before the fire, a novel open in her lap.

She has declared it a reading day, she says. Nothing else to do when the weather turns. "My bones are getting old," she says, "and they don't like the damp."

A ghoul sits in the other chair, unnoticed. A young man, little more than an elbow on a knee, a chin in a hand, mimicking Hannah's posture. Olivia tries to place him from the portrait hall, but there isn't enough of his face, and when he catches her looking, he dissolves into the velvet cushions. Olivia hugs the journals to her front and slips out, wondering how many ghouls there are at Gallant. One for every gravestone? Do the dead always come home?

Her feet carry her through the house, back to the music room.

Rain falls in a steady sheet beyond the bay window, making the rose heads droop, the distant wall blurred by weather and fog until it looks like an unfinished sketch. She half expects to see Matthew out there, kneeling among the flowers, head bowed despite the rain.

But there's no sign of him. Perhaps he is still in bed. She thinks of his face the night before, the exhausted slump of his shoulders, the shadows beneath his eyes, and hopes he has found sleep.

The piano sits, waiting, but Olivia resists the urge to sit on the bench again, stumbling across Matthew's melody, lest it wake him if he's resting. Instead, she sinks among the cushions on the window bench and spreads out the journals and the sketchpad.

They lie there like pieces in a puzzle, waiting to be solved.

I went beyond the wall, her mother wrote. *And I met Death.*

I did not tell my brother that the shadow let me go.

And then, *I wrote to him last night.*

Those words snag something in her. She turns to the first entry in the old green journal, even though the line is burned into her memory.

If you read this, I am safe.

It always struck her as a strange first entry. Now it strikes her as an introduction. She knows the "you" in the journal to be her father, based on the way her mother wrote to him, the way she mourned his loss.

Don't leave. Please, hold on a little longer. You cannot go before you meet her.

If that's true, then her father was the "tallest shadow," the one Grace claims she met beyond the wall. But there is nothing beyond the wall, as far as she can tell, and her father was not a figment of her mother's mind, a ghostly figure in a fairy tale—Olivia is proof that he was real. He lived and breathed. . . .

And wrote.

Olivia turns through the red journal until she finds the line.

. . . when I checked, I found that he had written back.

She frowns, looking from one journal to the other. She has read the green book a thousand times and found only her mother's sloping hand, her shifting thoughts. She turns through it again, searching for any sign of her father, and finds only the same entries and illustrations she knows by heart.

Frustration wells inside her, and she flings a cushion across the room.

What were you doing? she thinks, the words directed not at herself, but her mother. *What did you mean? Help me understand.*

A shadow twitches at the edge of her sight. A curtain of hair, caught in a breeze. A bare foot stepping soundless on the floorboards. Her mother. Olivia doesn't look up, afraid that if she does, the ghoul will disappear. She resists, even as the shape drifts near. Even as it sinks onto the window seat.

Olivia's heart thuds loud inside her chest. She has learned to ignore the ghouls or banish them by glaring, but it's never crossed her mind to call on them. Never occurred to her that they would come.

But her mother's ghoul sits beside her now, knees curled up beneath its chin, as if summoned. It is so young, and Olivia can't help but wonder if this is what Grace looked like when she died, or when she left, or younger still, when she first began to dream of freedom—which version of her came home to Gallant?

Out of the corner of her eye, she sees the ghoul lean forward as if to study the journals, watches it run a transparent hand almost lovingly over the illustration, ink blooming beneath its fingers. Its gaze—half-there, one side of its face crumbling to shadow—flicks up to Olivia. Its mouth—what's left of it—opens, as if trying to speak. No sound comes out. But its hand moves back and forth over the illustration.

Olivia studies the page through the veil of her mother's skin. And then something crackles through her. She reaches for the red journal and turns the pages back to the beginning, scanning the margins for one of the sketches her mother drew. They are so delicate, so precise—and so different from the inky blooms. As if they were not even made by the same hand. Two different styles. Two different artists.

Olivia looks down at the journal she's had all her life, and at last, she understands.

The words are her mother's voice.

The drawings are her father's.

If you read this, I am safe.

I lie awake and wonder why.

Why did you help me? Why do you stay in that place? Are you afraid to leave? Or are you bound to it, as I am bound, each of us prisoners in our house?

But a house like this will never be a home.

I dreamed of you last night. Isn't that strange? I dreamed that you were standing in the garden, looking up. I dreamed that you were waiting for the sun to rise. It never came.

What do you dream of, I wonder?

Do you even dream at all?

I had a bird once. I kept it in a cage. But one day someone let it go. I was so angry, then, but now I wonder if it was me. If I rose in the night, half-asleep, and slipped the lock and set it free.

Free—a small word for such a magnificent thing.

I don't know what it feels like, but I want to find out.

If I gave you my hand, would you take it?

If I ran, would you run with me?

Meet me here tomorrow night.

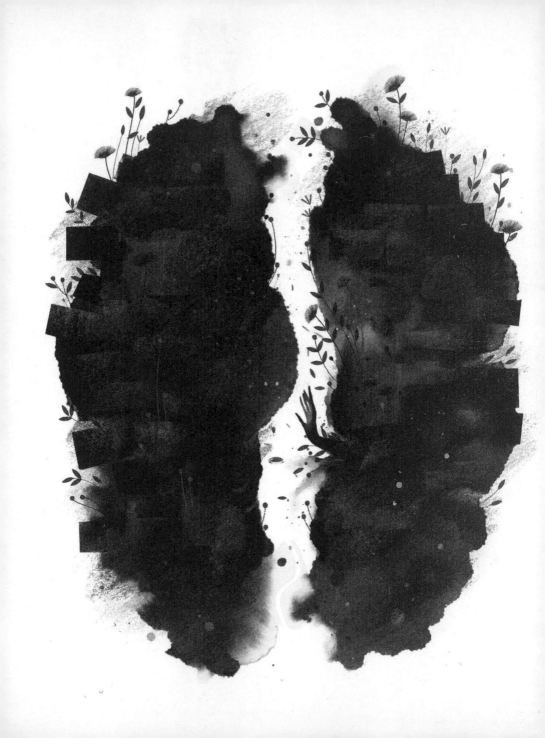

We did it. We did it.

We made it. We are free. And yet—

It doesn't feel real. I can't believe that you are sitting next to me, that I can reach out and touch your hand, that I can speak and you will hear. I suppose there is no need to write to you this way now. Perhaps I am writing for myself. It is a habit hard to shake.

I am so happy.

I am so scared.

The two, it turns out, can walk together, hand in hand.

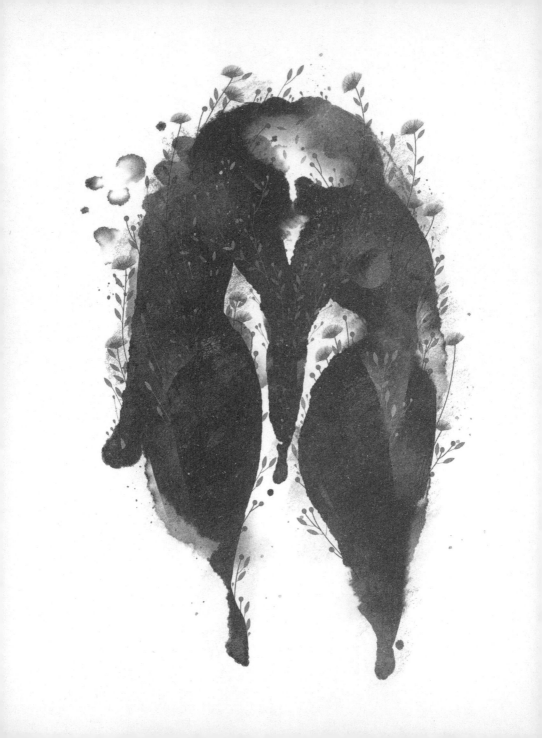

I can't believe it. But the world is full of stranger things, and I am giddy with the knowing.

What a marvel it is, to feel her heart in time with mine. What a wonder to know that she is there. What will we call her?

Olivia.

Home is a choice.

Something is wrong.

I grow wide, but you grow thinner by the day. I can see you withering. I am afraid tomorrow I will see straight through you. I am afraid the next, you will be gone.

I don't know how to make you better.
I don't know how to make you stay.
Stay with me. Stay with me. Stay with me.
I would write the words a thousand times if they'd be strong
enough to hold you here.

Don't leave. Don't leave. Please, hold on a little longer.
You cannot go before you meet her. Hold on. Hold on. Hold on.

I slept in your ashes last night.

It was like you laid your shadow down before you left. It smelled like hearth smoke and winter air. I made a blanket of the empty space. I pressed my cheek against the place where yours had been.

When you came apart, I found the cursed bone. It was a molar, of all things, his mouth hiding inside yours. But don't worry, I ground the tooth to dust and threw the filings on the fire. He will never have the piece that was you. I hope he rots while worrying the hole.

It was never this quiet when you were here. Isn't that funny? How much sound a body makes. I hate the silence, hate the fact that I'm the only one making noise. I make so much of it, as if I can trick myself into thinking you're here, just out of sight.

Perhaps you are haunting me.

What a comforting thought.

Maybe it's you in the darkness.

I swear I've seen it move.

The ashes are all gone now. I wish I'd kept the tooth.

Just to have something. At least I have Olivia. She is so quiet. She has your eyes, I think, but when I look at her I wonder if it's you staring back at me, or him. I hope it is not him but those eyes are so steady, so old for a child's face and I want to ask her if she knows if she sees if she belongs to that other place, but she is too young to speak.

I hear you in my dreams. Every night when I try to sleep I find myself back at the wall, and there you are, waiting on the other side. You bend your head to mine and whisper and that is how I know it is a lie. His voice in your mouth, telling me to come back, to come back, to come home.

There is no rest in sleep.

These dreams will be the death of me.

I feel like a pane of glass, shot through with cracks and every night the wind is buffeting. The splinters spread, the glass groans under the weight. It will break. I will break. It is only a matter of time and I am so so so tired ~~it is hard to know~~ sometimes I am sure I am awake, only to find myself waking and other times I am certain I'm asleep, only to drift off again. Time skips and my mind wanders and my feet carry me places when I am not looking I blink and I've moved the sun has moved the moon is up and Olivia sits there watching and ~~I don't know how long and~~ I want to rest so I won't be alone so I can see you ~~I can see you~~ and it makes me want to fall asleep but he always finds me there.

I don't remember falling asleep but I woke up and I was standing over Olivia whispering her name and I am afraid it wasn't my hand on her cheek wasn't my voice in my mouth wasn't my eyes watching her sleep ~~and~~

I am so tired I don't know what to do ~~it isn't safe but nowhere is~~ ~~safe now I am not here when~~ I'm awake and I am somewhere else ~~asleep I need to close my eyes but the shadows are moving I can see~~ ~~them when I am not looking and I am scared not of them but of me~~ ~~of the voice in the dark of the absence of you I am scared of what I'll~~ ~~do if I don't it doesn't matter I know it can't go on I can't go on and~~ I am sorry I wanted to be free ~~sorry I opened the door sorry you're~~ ~~not here and they are watching he is watching he wants you back but~~ ~~you are gone he wants me but I won't go he wants her but she is all I~~ ~~have of you and me she is all she is all~~ I want to go home.

Olivia Olivia Olivia

I have been whispering the name into your hair
~~so you will remember~~ will you remember?
~~I don't know I can't~~ They say there is love in
letting go but I feel only loss. My heart is ash and
~~did you know ash holds its shape until you touch it~~
I do not want to leave you but I no longer trust myself
~~there is no time there is no time there is no time to~~
I'm so sorry I don't know what else to do
Olivia, Olivia, Olivia, Remember this—
the shadows ~~cannot touch~~ are not real
the dreams ~~are only dreams~~ can never hurt you
and you will be safe as long as you stay away
from Gallant

The master of the house has not forgotten.

Every time his dry tongue slides over his polished teeth and dips into the groove, it is a spade driven into soil, the ground overturned, the memory made fresh.

A piece of him is missing. He cannot call it back.

Wrong, wrong. Things come together and fall apart, but he does not. He is the maker. He is the source. He lends, they borrow, but everything comes back.

He counts every sliver and every bone, he knows where they are when they are with him and when they are not, and he can call them home.

He snaps his fingers, and they skitter across the floor, fit themselves into the gaps, skin closing over every wound until only four remain.

Here is the place where the rib will go.

Here, the collar, here the wrist.

And here, the molar. The only wound that will not close. The master grinds his teeth.

A piece of him was stolen.

And soon he will have it back.

Part Four
BEYOND THE WALL

The longer she studies the journal, the more obvious it is.

The placement of the drawings. The way they disappear when he does.

Her mother's ghoul wavers at the edge of her sight, watching, wordless, as she turns through the green journal again, this time studying the inks as if they were letters, a correspondence played out in two forms, one line, the other shape. She tries to read them both, as if both are words, but the images are too abstract.

Why didn't he just write? she thinks, digging her thumbs into the soft space above her eyes. Perhaps he was like Matthew. And yet, he could discern her mother's hand well enough to answer. She imagines Grace Prior poring over the illustrations. *She* was clearly able to decipher them.

Olivia will, too.

She brushes her hand over her father's work, the ink as thin and wild as watercolor.

It is like watching clouds, trying to spot the shapes as they drift past, each one something and nothing at the same time, a promise of a picture more than the picture itself, but the longer she looks, the more her vision blurs, and the more her vision blurs, the more she seems to notice. Soon she stops trying to read the lines as shapes, and they become gestures. The images unfurl into sentiments. It is the difference between a language spoken and one signed, the mouth shaping words while the hands shape more, words and thoughts and feelings.

In her father's gestures, she reads relief and sadness, hope and longing.

There are pieces she doesn't understand, fragments that seem to dip out of reach, but it is a start. It is the first glimpse of a father she has never known, the ghost of him impressed on paper.

Olivia stops and stretches, feeling stiff. How long has she been at this? The rain is little more than mist now, and her eyes have begun to ache, so she closes the journal, running her hand almost absently over the twin grooves scraped into the front. And then, to her surprise, a ghostly hand falls over hers, and through. The ghoul's touch is nothing, a cool shadow—still, she jumps, jerking back on instinct, only to realize it wasn't reaching for her. Instead, its too-thin fingers drag through the air, tracing the same grooves in the cover of the book before drifting away. Olivia follows the ghoul's hand to the window, where it rests against the glass.

Olivia cannot help herself. She looks straight at her mother's ghoul, then, and for a moment—only a moment—she sees Grace

Prior, interrupted here and there by the watery gray light, her face where it shows a mask of sadness, eyes focused on the world beyond the window. At the garden. At the wall.

For a moment—only a moment—before the weight of Olivia's gaze grows too heavy, and the ghoul wavers and disappears.

Olivia leans forward, following the path those fingers made, from the journal to the window, where they hovered on the glass. As if reaching or pointing toward the garden and the wall.

Her gaze drops again to the dented green cover, those twin lines tugging something in her skull. She reaches for her sketchpad, turning through until she finds a drawing she made of the door in the wall, of the dark iron and its vine-shaped handle, of the gap where metal door met the surrounding stone. At the two bolts that stuck out, roughly the same distance apart as the marks on the front of the journal.

And then she's up and on her feet, moving through the house.

Past the sitting room where Hannah snores before a dying fire, and up the stairs. Down the hall—Matthew's door still shut—and into her mother's room. She finds a pair of yellow galoshes in the back of the wardrobe, stuffing socks into the toes until they fit, leaves the sketchpad on the bed, and tucks the red journal under her pillow, taking only the green one with her.

It's still light out, though for how long she can't be sure, so she moves briskly through the house and out the garden door.

The rain has stopped, but the wind is up and the air is wet, and the clouds still hang heavy and low, their undersides dark with the promise of another storm. She presses the journal against her front as she trudges past the roses and down the slope to the wall, slowing only when the door comes into sight.

Last night I went beyond the wall. And I met Death.

But her mother met her father, too.

Somehow, despite the weather, the door isn't even wet. The stone wall leans forward, just enough that the metal has stayed dry, and if Olivia weren't so consumed with her quest, she might think it strange, might add it to the way the shadows bent, even when the sun was out, to the cold air that gathers against the stone like mist.

A ghoul shudders at the orchard's edge. Not the old man, but her uncle, or at least, the pieces of him. She draws the rest in her mind, imagines him not as a specter, but a man, leaning, arms crossed against the nearest tree. The ghoul stares at her, and she stares back, but it doesn't dissolve under her gaze. It takes a step toward her, and Olivia finds herself thinking, *Stop*, thinking, *Stay there*, and to her surprise, it does.

The ghoul's face twitches, and it shifts back into the shadow of the trees, leaving her alone before the wall.

Olivia traces her fingers down the edge of the door, following the gap between the iron and the stone. Save for the two bolts jutting into the sliver of space, it is the width of a thumb. Or a journal spine. She bites her lip and slips her mother's journal between the door and the wall.

It is not the same shape it was, so many years ago.

It is a little wider now, the pages Anabelle once tore out returned imperfectly, age foxing the edges and warping the cover.

And yet, it fits. The green journal slides spine first into the gap with all the ease of a key in its lock, those two old bolts kissing their familiar grooves.

This is where her parents met.

This is how they spoke. Letters and drawings passed back and forth through a door that does not work in a wall that leads nowhere.

Olivia's fingers drop from the journal, and it sits there, resting comfortably in the gap for the length of an inhale. And then the world breathes out. The wind picks up. A sudden gust rustles her dress and tugs at her hair and knocks the journal from its perch.

If the wind had blown the other way, the journal would have tumbled toward her, fallen at her feet. But it blows at her back, and the journal tips through the gap, vanishing beyond the wall.

Olivia hisses through her teeth.

She pulls on the old door but of course it's locked, so she hurries to the edge of the wall, the place where the stone crumbles away to nothing, the grasses on either side growing together, this side tangling with that.

It is just a step, she tells herself.

And yet, she hesitates. Glances back over her shoulder at the garden and the looming house, Matthew's warning heavy on the air.

But she is not afraid of stories.

Sure, there are strange things in the world. Dead things that lurk in shadows. Houses full of ghosts. But this is just a wall, and standing here, at the edge, she can *see* the field beyond. Peering round the broken stone, she spots the journal lying in the wet grass, waiting to be retrieved.

Olivia takes a breath and rounds the wall.

Her borrowed yellow boot crosses the line, and it is the strangest thing, but in that moment, she thinks of the statue in the fountain, the woman's hand thrust out, not in welcome, but in warning, as if to say, Turn back, stay away. But the woman faces the world, not the wall, and Olivia's boot lands soundly on the ground.

It is one step.

A single stride between here and there, the side facing Gallant and the one facing the fields beyond. One step, and she half expects to feel some magic current, some errant breeze forcing her forward or buffeting her back, but the truth is, she feels nothing. No warning shift, no sudden plunge, no skin-crawling sense of a world gone wrong. Just the old familiar thrill of doing something you've been told not to.

Just to be sure, Olivia takes a step back, onto the garden side.

Nothing. How silly she feels then, like a child hopping between paving stones as if some are made of lava.

She crosses the wall again, glancing back over her shoulder at Gallant—still there, unchanged—before turning her attention to the world beyond. It looks the same. An empty field, an unkempt version of the grassy slope, her mother's green journal lying at the base of the wall where it fell. She marches toward it, but halfway there, another gust of wind kicks up. It flings the cover back, and steals the once-torn pages, scattering them across the still-damp grass.

Olivia lets out a silent yelp and chases after them.

One has snagged on a thistle nearby.

One has caught against a sturdy reed.

One she plucks out of the air as it sails past.

One lies dampened in the dirt.

The last has fallen farther out, in the field, and by the time she retrieves it, the hem of her blue dress is wet, her bare legs cold, her yellow galoshes slick with mud and leaves.

She trudges back to the wall, where the journal lies open, pages drifting back and forth in the breeze. She returns the damp and crumpled pages to the book, resolving to find tape or glue when she gets back to the house, to fix them in place.

It's getting late—or at least, she thinks it is; the low clouds have erased the line between day and dusk, making it impossible to tell the time—so she tucks the journal under her arm and hurries back to the edge of the wall, hoping no one has noticed her absence. Hoping that Hannah is still dozing by the fire, and Edgar is still humming in the kitchen, and Matthew is still asleep in his bed, and not at the piano, his eyes trained on the garden and the gate. The way his mood would darken if he saw her rounding the wall.

But when she gets to the edge of the stone, it isn't there.

Olivia looks up, confused.

It's roughly twelve strides from the wall's edge to the door—she measured—but she has walked that much, and now the crumbling edge hovers in the distance, another twelve ahead. She walks toward it, but with every stride, the wall grows longer, the end out of reach.

She breaks into a clumsy run, trying to outpace the stone, but it is always one step ahead. It goes on and on, and Olivia slows, breathless, panic worming through her limbs.

She twists round, intending to head back for the iron gate.

And stops.

The field is gone. There is no tall grass. No thistles. No wild world.

In its place, there is a garden.

Or at least, the shriveled remains of a garden. Withered limbs and wilting blooms, their petals pale, their leaves devoid of color. There is an orchard to one side, its branches bare, and the remains of a vegetable patch to the other, its contents long gone to seed and rot.

And there, at the top of the ruined garden, sits another Gallant.

Chapter Seventeen

Once, back at Merilance, Matron Sarah held a drawing class.

Olivia had already begun to teach herself—a habit started early. There was a kind of power in capturing the world around her, distilling it to lines and curves, a language of gestures that anyone could understand.

But in this class, the girls were told to draw themselves.

The matron gave each a sheet of paper and a pencil and showed them how to render their own face, how to measure the distance of their eyes, the angle of their nose and cheeks and smile. And then she set them loose.

A small stack of mirrors lay in the center of the table, some new and others silvered, some cracked and others whole. There weren't enough to go around, so the girls had to share, stealing glimpses of themselves whenever they could, which meant the angles and the light were always changing, and when the time was up, and the portraits tacked on the wall, the room was full of faces, and every one of them was *wrong*.

A distorted reflection, strange, unnerving.

That is what Olivia sees when she looks at the house beyond the wall.

It has all the right features, arranged the wrong way. A drawing done too much from memory or a contour sketch, where you do not lift the pen, and all the lines connect and bleed together into something abstract, a stylized impression.

Overhead, the dusk has somehow dropped away, the sky an inky black. There is no moon. No stars. And yet, it is not empty. No, it is like a lake, a vast expanse of dark water. The kind of dark that tricks the eye. Makes you see things where there are none. Or miss things when they are there. The dark that lives in the spaces you know you should not look, lest you catch sight of other eyes, staring back.

Olivia retreats, pressing herself back against the wall, expecting stone, and shivering when she feels the kiss of iron instead. The door.

She pushes, but it doesn't move. She searches for a keyhole—but there's not even a handle, nothing but a film of debris on the metal, dead ivy and leaves that flake away like rust or skin.

She presses her eye to the narrow gap and sags with relief when she sees Gallant—the *real* Gallant—still sitting on the other side, dusk settling over the garden. Her mind goes to the strange metal sculpture in the study, the two houses facing each other across the twisting spheres.

A shadow moves across a window—Hannah—and Olivia pounds on the door, expecting the sound to carry, to echo, but it doesn't. The iron swallows the noise like silk, or down, or moss. And as she watches, Hannah lifts one hand to close the shutter. Locking out the dark. And her.

Olivia takes a step back and feels the small crunch of something beneath her boot.

Looking down, she finds a handful of small white seeds scattered at her feet. She bends to take one up, feels the point between her finger and thumb and realizes they are not seeds at all, but tiny *teeth*. She looks around and sees a handful of other bones, thin and brittle. Bits of beak and paw and wing, and her first thought is, here are all the animals she should have heard and seen at Gallant.

She doesn't realize her hand has closed over the little tooth until it *jumps*. Shudders like a bee against her palm. Olivia gasps, cold prickling up her arm as she lets go, and by the time it hits the ground, it is not a writhing bit of bone, but a *mouse*.

A small, gray-furred thing that skitters away into the wasted garden.

Olivia stares down at her palm, now empty, and wonders what the hell is happening, if she fell in the field and hit her head. If this is yet another dream.

She looks up at the house that is not Gallant.

The shutters hang open, and a pale glow suffuses the windows. A light is on somewhere inside.

She hovers for a moment, uncertain what to do, wishing she had more than a journal in her hands, but knowing she can't stay here, standing like a solitary tree beneath that eerie sky, exposed. She cannot go back, it seems, and so at last, her feet carry her forward.

The ground rustles like dry paper under her boots, too loud in the silent garden. Even the wind seems to hold its breath as she creeps forward, her yellow galoshes practically glowing against the charcoal world. (She cannot tell if the night has rendered this place colorless, or if there truly is no color in it.)

All around her, wilted flowers droop on thin, stiff stems, roses look as if a single breath would send the petals scattering, and branches stand bare save for leaves that look as though they died in place. All of it brittle, wasted.

A fragile rose leans into her path, and Olivia brushes her fingertips across the petals, expecting them to crack and crumble. Instead, she feels a sudden prickle in her hand, like the promise of pain the instant a knife slips and cuts, the moment before you bleed. She jerks back, studying her fingertips, but there is no wound, only a strange chill creeping across her skin. She shivers and shakes out her hand.

And then she sees the plant she touched, no longer dead, but blooming, wild. New blossoms force their way up and out, a season's growth in a matter of moments. Olivia watches, stunned, torn between the urge to flee and the longing to run her hands over the other flowers, just to watch them grow. Only two things stop her: the cold that lingers on her skin; and the way the rose leans forward, as if reaching, hungry.

She backs away, turns her attention to the looming house. There is the small door, sitting at the top of the slope, or she can round the garden and the house, climb the steps to the wide front doors and knock and wait to see what answers.

The thought makes her shiver, fingers tightening on the battered green book.

She heads for the garden door, stopping only to slip off the yellow boots, the rubber and the color both as loud as voices in this silent place. The blue of her dress is just as bright, but there's nothing to be done for that. She is setting the boots by the door when something moves in the garden to her left. She feels more than hears it and turns round, eyes scanning the darkened grounds.

A ghoul stands amid the ruined flowers.

A woman, maybe Hannah's age.

Olivia can see through the specter, here and there, like a tattered curtain, but there is more to it than just an elbow or a cheek. It has limbs and legs, and in one hand, a *dagger*. And when Olivia looks right at the ghoul, it doesn't disappear. Doesn't even wane or waver. It just stares back, and there is something familiar in the set of its jaw, the line of its brow. But it's the look on its face that chills Olivia. *Fear.*

She glances past it, one last time, down the garden to the wall, the door shut fast, the edges blurring into fog, and then Olivia reaches for the garden door. She brings her hand to the knob, expecting it to soften and crumble, give way to ash, or smoke, a phantom door in a phantom house. But it holds firm against her fingers. The handle turns. The door swings open.

She steps into the house.

And realizes she isn't sure what to do.

She thought the answer would rise to meet her when she crossed the threshold, like dust shaken free. But the door is a door, and the hall beyond is a hall, and when she looks around, she sees a drearier, colorless version of the Gallant she knows, but otherwise, there is nothing. No one.

And yet, she does not *feel* alone.

She clutches the green journal to her chest, wishing she'd brought the other book, the red one from the time before, and tries to remember her mother's words.

The tallest shadow found me in the hall.

The shadow was her father. He wanted to help—he showed her mother the way out. Perhaps someone will come to help her too.

Perhaps—but she is not about to stand around and wait for it.

Her bare feet find their way across the floor.

Olivia Prior has never been a quiet girl. She has always made a point of making noise, everywhere she goes, in part to remind people that just because she cannot speak, does not mean that she is silent, and in part because she simply likes the weight of sound, likes the way it takes up space.

But now, as she pads barefoot through the house that is not Gallant, she makes herself quiet, silent, small. Folds in all her edges and holds her breath as she makes her way down the hall to the front foyer, the twisting circles inlaid in the floor.

She looks up, searching the grand stairs for the light she saw from the garden, but there's no source. Instead, that faint glow seems to come from everywhere, not lantern bright, more like moonlight. As if someone took the roof away and hung the pale white sphere right overhead.

It is just enough to see by, but not enough to see well. And yet, even in the dark, one thing is clear.

This house is falling down. Not fading quietly, like Gallant, slipping slowly with neglect. No, this house is *crumbling* around her.

The small cracks she saw on the other side, the peeling paper and the ceiling damp, here those things are magnified. Floorboards are broken. A fault line runs up a wall, deep enough to fit her fingers in. In the sitting room, the stone around the hearth has splintered, pieces of rock and mortar piled on the floor. The whole house feels as if it's collapsing in slow motion. As if one wrong step or nudge might bring the whole thing down.

And the sight of it is not frightening, but *sad*.

She can't shake the feeling she's been here before, which in a sense, she has. But it is not just the warped reflection of the other house that has her so unnerved. It is the taste, perhaps, or the smell, or some unquantifiable thing, a sense memory, something inside her saying *yes*, saying *here*, saying *home*.

What a horrifying thought.

It clings like cobwebs, and she shivers, pushing it away as she turns down a corridor she knows: the portrait hall. But there are no paintings here, no frames. The walls are empty, the paper not peeling but shredded, as if by fingernails. The door at the end hangs open, and there on the floor, she sees the grand piano slumped and broken. As if its legs gave way and sent the whole thing crashing down. As if it lay there for a hundred years, until the lid warped and the keys fell out like teeth.

Her feet carry her forward, and she kneels to rest her good hand on the broken instrument. A strange thought, then, of the mouse and the flowers, and she presses her palm flat to the piano's side as if her touch alone can bring it back.

She waits—for what? For the prickle, the chill, for the piano to rise and put itself back together, but it doesn't, and she feels only foolish, her hand slipping away. A shadow twitches, and Olivia's head jerks up.

A ghoul stands at the bay window, facing the garden, the wall. A swatch has been torn out of him, a ribbon erasing one shoulder and part of his chest, but silver light traces what is left, and when he turns his head, her heart lurches. She knows his face. Saw it in the portrait hall at Gallant, the very first picture. Alexander Prior.

He looks at her, and there is such fury in his eyes that she recoils, backing out of the room, into the hall.

And then she hears it.

Not voices or music, but *movement*. Ghouls make no sound

when they move, but humans do. They make a lot of noise, simply being. They breathe, and they walk, and they touch, and all of it creates noise, the kind you hardly notice over the louder, ringing sounds like laughter and speech.

When she cranes to listen, she hears a rhythm, the tap and slide of bodies moving through space, the hush of it like wind through trees.

Olivia follows the sound down one hall and up another, until she reaches the double doors that lead into the ballroom. The one she spun across in the other house, bare feet whispering on inlaid wood.

These doors hang open, a crescent of silver spilling into the hall, and when she peers around the corner she sees—

Dancers.

Two dozen of them, twirling around the room, and the first thing she realizes is that they are not ghouls. They are not threadbare and broken, are not missing pieces, not caught between the shadow and the light.

They are *people*. In the low silver light, they look as though they've been drawn in shades of gray. Their clothes. Their skin. Their hair. Everything painted in the same colorless palette, and yet, they are lovely. As she watches, they pair off and turn, break apart and pair again, moving through the motions of the dance, and the whole time, they move in silence.

The men's shoes and the women's skirts murmur across the wooden floor, the rustle of bodies moving through space, but there is no music pouring through the hall, no soft chatter between partners, just the eerie whisper of the dance.

The first real sound she hears is the steady rap of a finger on wood. A hand keeping time. Olivia follows the *tap-tap-tap* past the dancers to the front of the room, where a man sits in a high-backed chair.

A man, and not a man.

He is not a ghoul, but he looks nothing like the dancers, either. Where they are the gray of pencil sketches, he is drawn in ink. Dressed in a high-collared coat, his hair the black of wet soil, his skin the off-white of ashes gone cold, and his eyes—

His eyes.

His eyes are the flat and milky white of Death.

Chapter Eighteen

Tap. Tap. Tap. Tap.

I went beyond the wall.

Tap. Tap. Tap. Tap.

And I met Death.

Tap. Tap. Tap. Tap.

He raps one finger as the dancers dip and twirl, their dizzy circle so like the sculpture in the study, the single push that sent it spinning.

The man who is not a man looks somehow ancient but not *old.* His skin is not creased, yet here and there it peels away, the polished bone beneath showing through like stone under thinning ivy. And that is how she sees that there are pieces of him missing—not lost to shadow, like the ghouls, but carved away.

The joint of one finger. The edge of one cheek. A collarbone splintered at the neck of his shirt. The skin has been flayed back around each injury, and yet, he does not seem to be in pain.

Just . . . bored.

A twitch of movement on the platform, and Olivia tears her

gaze from the stranger in the high-backed chair and sees that he is not alone.

Three figures stand about him, as gray as the dancers, but rendered darker, a draftsman's hand pressed harder to the page, and dressed not like revelers but knights, a suit of armor shared between them.

The first is built like a brick, sturdy and stout, a steel pauldron bound across his shoulder.

The second is built like a whisper, willow thin, a plate of metal on their chest.

The third is built like a wolf, short and strong, a gauntlet gleaming on her hand.

They range around the high-backed chair, the stout one grim-faced behind the throne, the thin one just beside it, the short one on her haunches against the wall. And even though they are fully there, even though they have garments and faces, they remind her of nothing so much as shadows cast at different times of day.

They watch the dance without watching, the faraway look of the weary and the tired and the unimpressed as their master taps, keeping time with a music only he can hear.

And then, with a sudden jerk, he rises.

Unfolds from his chair and steps down among the dancers. They part and twirl, and as he moves between them, one by one, they die. It is not a human death—there is no blood, no scream. They simply crumble, like petals dropping from long dead flowers, bodies breaking into ash as they hit the floor.

The master of the house does not seem to notice.

Does not seem to care.

His dead-white eyes only watch as they fall to every side, collapsing in a silent, terrible tide, until there is only one dancer left. Her partner has just crumbled, and she looks down at the dust covering her dress and blinks, as if waking from a spell. She sees the ruins of the ball, the creature moving toward her, and her face, which had until now been a mask of calm, begins to break into confusion, into fear. Her mouth opens in a silent gasp, a plea. He reaches for her hand, and she shuffles back, but it is not enough. He catches her wrist and draws her close.

"Now, now," he says, and his voice isn't loud, but there is nothing for it to overcome, and so it carries like a crack of thunder through the hollow room. "I would never hurt *you*."

The dancer doesn't believe him, not at first. But then the master sweeps her back into the motions of the dance, the two of them turning in elegant circles through the ashes of the fallen, and with each step, she relaxes a little more into her role, letting him lead, until the fear ebbs from her face, the steady calm resumes.

And then he stops dancing and lifts her chin and says, "See?"

And she is just beginning to smile when he says, "Enough," and the word is as swift and violent as a breath on a candle, snuffing it out.

The dancer crumbles against him, her body sagging into ash, and he sighs.

"Honestly," he says, brushing the dust from his front, as if annoyed that it might stain. A pale white fragment shines on the wooden floor where the dancer stood, and at first Olivia thinks it is a slip of paper or a seed. But then it rises and tucks itself against the tear along his jaw, and she realizes it was a shard of *bone.*

A sound fills the room, like rattling, like rain, as more bones skitter over the floor. They rise from the ashes of each fallen body, fragments no bigger than a knuckle, a thumbnail, a tooth. The master stands at the center of it all, waiting as the slivers shudder and draw toward him, fitting themselves back into the places where his skin had peeled away.

It is like a cup breaking in reverse. A hundred brittle shards returning to their porcelain surface, rebuilding the pattern, erasing the cracks. Olivia watches, half in horror, half in awe, as paper-white skin closes over the bones, watches as the man who is not a man rolls his head on his shoulders as if working out a kink, watches as he spins on his heel, turning toward the armor-clad soldiers on the platform, the only ones still there.

"Anyone care for a dance?" he asks with a flourish.

They stare back at him, one grim, one sad, one bored. But they say nothing.

His face flickers, quick as a candle between anger and amusement. "None of you are any fun these days," he says, marching across the ballroom to the balcony doors. He flings them open and steps out into the dark.

This whole time, Olivia has been holding her breath.

Now, at last, she lets it out. It makes almost no sound, just a small exhale, the faintest whoosh of air. But the dancers are all gone, the other sounds gone with them, and in the silence, even a breath makes too much noise.

A head twitches toward the open door.

It's one of the soldiers. The short one balanced on her haunches at the platform's edge. Her head swivels, dark eyes shifting to the ballroom door just as Olivia retreats into the safety of the hall. She presses herself flat into the pool of dark behind one of the doors, squeezing her eyes shut and hoping that she was fast enough, that when the shadow looked her way, it saw nothing. That by the time it scanned the open doors, she was already gone. She clutches her mother's journal and tries to disappear into the wall of the house.

Olivia has never been the sort to pray.

Back at Merilance, she was told to kneel and knit her fingers and speak to a God she couldn't see, couldn't hear, couldn't touch. She didn't want to get her knuckles rapped, so she knelt, and she knit her fingers and pretended.

She has never believed in higher powers, because if there were higher powers then they took her father and mother, they took her voice, they left her in Merilance with nothing but a book. But there are lower powers, stranger ones, and there in the dark, behind the door, she prays to them.

She prays for help—right until she hears the sound of boots, loud as bells on the ballroom floor. The clank of a hand flexing inside its gauntlet, the scrape of a blade sliding free of its sheath. Right until she sees the shadow cut across the moonlit floor.

And then, she runs.

She goes the wrong way. It isn't her fault—she knows she should have run for the front door, but she'd have had to step right into the soldier's path, so instead she flees farther down the hall, away from the door, and into the heart of the house.

Her steps are too loud, her breath is too loud, everything is too loud. And there is a wolf on her heels.

She reaches the room at the end of the hall, bursts into the study, slamming the door shut behind with a deafening *crack*. She drags a wooden chair before the door and manages to wedge it there, then spins, scouring the study for somewhere to hide, knowing there is nothing, knowing she is trapped. She has chosen the room without windows, without exits.

Nothing but broken shelves and the old wood desk.

The sculpture lies against the wall, as if someone flung it there. The rings are warped, the houses trapped beneath the twisted metal. Olivia starts toward it, hoping to pry away a piece of steel, anything to wield. She tucks the journal under her arm and kneels, picking at the ruined sculpture. Her wounded palm aches as she takes hold, trying to free something, anything, from the heap to use against the coming soldier.

Only, it doesn't seem to be coming anymore.

Her pulse pounds in her ears, and she strains to hear around it. She rises from the mess of metal, creeps back to the door, presses her ear to the wood and hears . . . nothing. Olivia sags, hoping that it is gone, that it was never there, that it didn't see her in the doorway, didn't follow her into the hall and—

A boot slams against the door, rattling the wood.

Olivia staggers back and turns, toes catching on the edge of the threadbare rug.

She trips and falls, knocking the wind from her lungs and banging her knees hard against the wooden floor. She throws out her hands to break her fall, and the journal tumbles and skids beneath the desk. The door rattles and shakes, and she scrambles toward the desk, reaching her arm long beneath it, fingers skimming the cover as the wood begins to splinter at her back.

A door groans open.

Not the study door but another, a small one hidden in the wall, where the bookshelves give way to curling paper. Olivia doesn't see the door swing open, doesn't see the ghoul that steps out of the hidden room until it wraps its rotting arms around her waist and hauls her back, away from the journal and the desk and the study and the splintering door.

Olivia kicks and twists and tries to fight free. It is no use.

The ghoul holds tight and drags her out of the study.

Into the dark.

Chapter Nineteen

Once upon a time, Olivia Prior was afraid of ghouls.

She was only five when she first began to notice them. One day the shadows were empty, and the next they weren't. The ghouls didn't appear all at once. It was like stepping out of the sun into a darkened room—her eyes had to adjust. One day she dropped a bit of chalk beneath the bed, knelt down, and found an open mouth. The next, a half-formed hand drifted past her on the stairs. A few days later, an eye floated in the black behind the door.

Over time, they took shape, knit themselves together from bits of skin and bone into the rough shapes she came to know as ghouls. They were the stuff of nightmares, and for weeks she didn't sleep, her back to the wall and her eyes on the dark.

Go away, she'd think, and they would, but they always came back. She didn't know why they followed her, didn't know why no one else could see them, was afraid that they were real and afraid that they weren't, afraid what the matrons would do if they found out that she was haunted or mad. But most of all, she was afraid of the ghouls themselves.

Afraid that they would reach out of the dark and grab her, ruined fingers closing over skin. And then one day she flung her hand out in frustration, expecting to meet dead flesh or at least the eerie brush of cobwebs, the mist of something halfway formed. But she felt nothing.

Gruesome as they were, they were not *there*.

Sure, she could see them from the corner of her eye, an unpleasant echo, like staring at the sun and having to spend an hour blinking away light. But she learned to ignore them because they could not touch her.

They could *never* touch her.

And yet, now, pressed back against a moldering wall in a hidden passage of the house that is not Gallant, she can *feel* the ghoul's hand over her mouth. And it is not the hint of a hand, not spider silk or mist, but long-rotten fruit and too-dry sticks, a bone-dry palm forced tight over her lips.

If she could scream, she would.

But she can't, so she fights, tries to force the ghoul off, fingers sinking through tattered cloth and hollow ribs, but the ghoul only twists her round and leans in close, its ruined face inches from her own, and in the silver dark, there's no menace in its filmy eyes, only a silent plea to be still.

Past her pounding heart, Olivia tries to listen to the room beyond the wall. She hears the splinter of the door, the steady beat of the soldier's boots as it crosses the study, passing from the wood onto the thin rug. She pictures its narrow, wolfish frame as it stalks around the desk. A knee touching down, and the metal gauntlet scraping the ground, and then—no. The soft drag of something being freed, the flutter of loose paper. Her mother's journal. Olivia's hands ache and her lungs burn. She has to go back for it, but she can't, she can't, so instead, she breathes against the rotting fingers, inhaling dead leaves and ash.

Until at last, the steps withdraw.

The silence drags long and flat.

The ghoul's palm falls away.

It retreats a step, and in the eerie almost-light that permeates the house, she sees it is—or was—a man, her uncle's age, perhaps, the same strong jaw and deep-set eyes she's come to know as Prior.

Its hands drift up in surrender, or perhaps apology. She doesn't understand, not until the fingers trace through the air, in something that is not sign language—not the kind she learned—but the gestures are slow, readable.

You . . . asked . . . for . . . help.

Olivia stares at the ghoul. She did, when she was hiding in the hall. But it was only a thought, a prayer, a silent plea, neither spoken nor signed.

How did you hear me? she asks, but the ghoul's attention twitches back toward the hidden door. Its face contorts, and then it gestures down the darkened passage.

You must go, it says. *The shadow is coming back.*

The shadow? she asks, but the ghoul turns her round to face the narrow hall. The dim silver light doesn't seem to reach more than a foot. Beyond, the darkness is a wall.

A ruined hand drifts past her as it points.

That way.

But her eyes hang on the withered hand. Olivia turns back. The mouse. The flowers. Twice she's touched the dead and brought them back to life, and so she reaches out to touch the ghoul's broken chest, but it catches her wrist and shakes its head.

Why not? she thinks.

Its other hand drags through the air. *Not yours.*

She doesn't understand, but the ghoul doesn't give her time to ask again. It turns her away from the hidden door and the wolf lurking beyond, and even though she cannot see it now, she can feel the warning in its touch. *Go.*

Thank you, she thinks, and the ghoul's fingers tighten on her shoulder. A single, brief squeeze, and then she is nudged forward. Down the corridor.

Ahead, the darkness is as thick as paint, and she half expects to feel it hold against her fingers. But when she takes a step, the wall draws back, the silver light moving with her, reaching only a few inches ahead. She brings her hand to the walls, the passage narrow enough that she can touch both sides with elbows bent.

She looks back, but the ghoul is gone.

Step by step, she feels her way forward, hands skating over old stone, hoping nothing else reaches out of the dark.

At last, she finds the other door.

She hesitates, unsure where it leads, if she's about to step out into the ballroom or the foyer. She presses her ear to the wood and listens for something, anything, on the other side, and hears nothing. A soft push, and the door whispers open onto the narrow alcove just outside the kitchen.

Like everything else in this house, it is the same, and not at all.

A deep crack runs across one wall. The floorboards rise and fall, as if roots are pushing up beneath them. There are no pots on the stove, no bread on the table, no smell of stew or toast or anything but ash, as if a heavy layer has settled over everything. A single apple sits on the splintered counter, withered and dry, the ghost of long, thin fingers left in the dust beside it.

Fear prickles up her spine.

In her mind, those same fingers tap on the edge of a chair, bone showing through torn white skin. Those fingers catch a dancer's wrist and draw her in. Those fingers brush her death away like dust.

Olivia drags her gaze to the small side door by the pantry, a glass insert looking out onto the night. Not the garden unraveling behind the house, but the front drive, the fountain, the road beyond.

She rushes toward the narrow door, and in five steps she is there, bursting out of the house and into the night like a body coming up for air. She doesn't know where to go, back to the impossible wall or down the empty road, but one has already refused her, so she decides to try the other. She starts across the drive, the gravel biting into her bare feet. *Shh, shh, shh,* it says, *too loud,* as she hurries past the fountain, where the stone woman looms, her outstretched hand broken off, her billowing dress in tatters, rocks littering the empty pool and—

But it's not empty.

There, on the floor of the fountain, lies a boy.

Chapter Twenty

A boy.

Not the *ghoul* of a boy, but a real one, flesh and blood and whole, his edges firm. He is Olivia's age, perhaps a year or two younger, with tawny hair that falls across his face. He looks as if he simply climbed into the fountain, curled up on the cold stone, and went to sleep. If it weren't for the silver cast to his skin, the way his wrists are bound together with dark ivy, the tendrils coiling around the statue's feet.

If it weren't for the fact he isn't moving.

She saw a dead body once. It was in the road, two winters back, a husk of a woman who'd folded in like a leaf in the frost and never got up. She looked like she was sleeping, too, but her limbs were stiff, skin sagging over bones, the spark of life so clearly gone.

No, the boy in the fountain isn't dead.

That is what she tells herself as she leans forward. As her fingers skim the air over his ankle, where the weedy ropes bind tight. But she can't quite reach. She is about to swing her leg over the stone lip of the fountain when she feels movement, hears the grind of gravel underfoot, and looks up, hoping to find another ghoul, before she remembers—ghouls make no noise.

There is a soldier standing in the drive.

The whip-thin one, armor plate gleaming on their chest. Their eyes are dark, almost mournful, but there is no mercy in them. Light twitches on the crumbling front steps, and she sees the second soldier sitting there, the brick of a man with the shining pauldron on his shoulder. He slouches, bored, elbows on knees and hands hanging loose and large as spades.

Olivia takes a step back, away from the fountain and the boy curled at the statue's feet, as something moves to her right and she catches the glint of a gauntlet as the third soldier steps out from behind the stone woman, smiling like a wolf.

The broad one stands.

The other two drift forward.

Metal glints on their hips, but they draw no weapons.

Somehow, that makes it worse. Their bare hands twitch. Their black eyes shine.

You asked for help, said the ghoul in the study, even though she only thought the word. Now, she thinks it again. *Help.*

It feels so small, unspoken, unsigned, less a word than a whisper, a breath.

Help, she thinks as the shadows stalk toward her. *Help, help, help . . .*

And then, they come.

Three ghouls emerge, not from the house or the garden or the dark. They rise straight up through the ground itself, sprouting like weeds between the gravel: a young man and a weathered woman, and then the one she saw in the music room, the first of the Priors. And though their bodies are broken, cleaved apart by darkness, and though there is no shine of metal on their clothes, she can tell they were dressed for battle, once.

They come, as if summoned, their bodies arranging into a shield before her.

The soldiers frown, the broad one perplexed, the thin one annoyed, the short one sneering as the young man's ghoul steps forward, empty hands spread wide. And though the ghouls say nothing, she can feel their order ringing through her bones.

Run.

Olivia lunges back toward the boy in the fountain, but the ghoul of the weathered woman catches her arm and shakes its head, pushes her away.

And then a blade sings through the ghoul's back, and it staggers, and Olivia knows the ghoul cannot die, knows it is already dead, but the sight of the metal spilling out of its chest, its knees buckling silently to the dirt, still sends a shock of horror through her bones.

The ghouls are no match for the soldiers. They have only bought her time.

And so, she runs, the only way she can, not down the empty road, but back toward the garden. A desperate sprint, driven only by the need to get away. Away from the house. Away from the soldiers with their glinting armor. Away, her blue dress snagging on bramble and thorn, her bare feet singing over the carpet of dead grass that runs between the withered garden and the barren orchard.

Away and back to the wall that will not end, the door that will not open. Almost there when a jagged root catches her toes and sends her tumbling, pain lancing through her hands and knees as she hits the ground. The fall knocks all the air from her lungs, but her pulse is a drum inside her head. *Get up, get up, get up.* And as she digs her hands into the cold damp earth to push herself up, she feels the poke of tiny sticks beneath her palms, and realizes too late that they are not sticks, but bones, the littered remains before the wall. Too late, she feels the prickling pain, the twitch of movement against her skin. Too late, the ground beneath her becomes a writhing carpet of paws and fur and wings, all of them alive.

Olivia scrambles back, a cold chill rolling up her arms.

Get away, she thinks, *get away,* and the crows take flight, and the mice scatter, and the rabbits bolt, and she forces herself to her feet, a sucking cold flooding through her limbs as she staggers to the garden door and throws herself against it.

The iron shudders, but doesn't give.

She pounds on it again, but the sound goes nowhere, ending right where her fists meet the metal, swallowed up like a scream into a soft down pillow.

Olivia sags against the door, breathless. And then she turns and puts her back to the cold metal and trains her eyes on the dark. Perhaps it is some primal need to face her fate, the same force that drives a girl to look beneath her bed, the knowledge that what you can't see is always worse than what you can.

She turns and looks at the house that isn't Gallant.

And sees him, looking back.

The master of the house stands on the balcony, elbows draped over the rail, his black coat billowing in the cold night air, and even from here she can see his milk-white eyes, watching her. Even from here, she can see the smile that parts his ashen face, can see his hand drift up and his too-thin finger crook into a single, chilling gesture, wordless but clear.

Come here.

There is no moon, but down in the garden, silver light shines on a shoulder, a chest, a hand. The soldiers are coming. They amble toward her, wild but silent, stalking her through the dark, and Olivia decides she is not ready to face her fate. She turns to the door in the wall and slams her fists against it again and again, until debris flakes away from the surface, exposing the iron beneath.

Open, open, open, she thinks, pounding until she can feel the searing heat of the cut on her hand as it reopens, can feel the blood welling on her skin, the pain ringing through her palm as it hits iron, and then there is a sound, deep inside the metal, like the end of a music note, more hum than noise. A lock groaning free.

The door in the wall swings open, and Olivia stumbles through, out of one night and into another. Out of the dead garden and onto damp green grass that soaks her knees as she collapses to the ground on the other side, gasping for air. Air that tastes like summer rain instead of ashes. Air that tastes of flowers and life and moonlight.

Footsteps race through the garden, and Olivia drags her head up in time to see Matthew running toward her, knife in hand. For a second, she thinks he means to kill her. There *is* murder in his eyes, his knuckles white on the weapon's hilt, but then she sees the blade's damp edge, the blood already dripping from his fingers. He surges past her to the open door.

She twists round and sees the shadows coming, sees darkness spilling through the open door and over the ground like oil, staining the dirt, before Matthew slams the iron shut, metal clanging over his voice as he says, "With my blood, I seal this door."

The door hums, the bolt groans home.

Olivia looks down at her aching palm, the cut split open, a fresh and angry line of red.

With my blood.

Matthew's hand is pressed flat to the iron, head bowed against the door. He breathes heavily, shoulders heaving. Olivia stands, about to reach for him, when he turns and grabs her shoulders, fingers digging deep enough to bruise.

"What have you done?" he demands, voice shaking.

And Olivia looks from her cousin to the wall and back again, wishing she could answer.

Wishing she knew.

It is all so loud inside the house.

Beyond the wall, everything was made of whispers, the eerie quiet magnifying every breath or step. But here, Hannah crashes about the kitchen, boiling water and gathering gauze, and Matthew won't stop shouting, even though he looks like he's about to faint, and Edgar drags up a stool and orders him to sit. The noise is like a tide, and Olivia lets it wash over her, grateful for the sound after so much silence, even if none of them are talking about what she saw, about the fact there is another world beyond the wall.

"How *dare* you," demands Matthew, and for once the words are lobbed at Hannah instead of her.

"I was only trying to help," she snaps back.

"Sit down," says Edgar.

"You *drugged* me."

Olivia startles, realizes that is why his bedroom door stayed closed, why she didn't see him.

"Better drugged than dead!" shouts Hannah, and Olivia cannot blame the woman. She saw his face the night before, the exhausted slump of his shoulders, the deep hollows beneath his eyes. "You needed rest."

"There is no rest!" he screams. "Not in this house."

"Sit *down*," orders Edgar as Matthew paces, a dishtowel wrapped around his hand, the cotton soaking red. He cut too fast, too deep, a vicious wound across his palm, and despite the cloth, a few fat red drops still find their way onto the kitchen floor.

With my blood, he said.

Olivia's own palm is in a sorry state, but Edgar has wrapped it in clean gauze (he would not even look at her), and her mind is not on the dull ache of her hand or the pain in the soles of her bare feet from running over gravel and broken earth, or the chill that lingers beneath her skin. Her mind is not here in the kitchen at all, but a hundred yards away at the garden's edge. Behind her eyes, she sees the corpses of small creatures rising at her touch, feels herself dragged into the darkness by dead hands, watches two dozen dancers turn to ash, bits of bone rattling on the ballroom floor as they skitter back to their master.

Edgar finally gets Matthew to sit.

"You had no right," he seethes at Hannah, but his eyes are fevered, his skin at once sallow and too pink, and she cannot help but think that despite his size, a decent wind would knock him over.

And Hannah is having none of it.

"I saw you born, Matthew Prior," she says. "I will not watch you kill yourself."

"You watched my father do it," he says, such venom in his voice that Hannah flinches. "You let my brother—"

"Enough!" shouts Edgar, decent, soft-voiced Edgar, the word landing like a blow on Matthew's cheek.

"Some days," says Hannah, voice brittle, "you are still such a child."

Matthew's eyes go dark as pitch. "I am a Prior," he says with a defiant scowl. "I was born to die in this house. But I'll be damned if that death is for nothing." He rounds then, leveling the full force of his anger at Olivia. "Pack your things. I never want to see your face again."

She recoils as if struck. Anger floods like heat beneath her skin.

I am a Prior, too, she wants to tell him. *I belong here as much as you. I have seen things you cannot see and done things you cannot do, and if you had told me the truth instead of treating me like a stranger in your house, then maybe I wouldn't have gone across. Maybe I could have helped.*

She lifts her hands to sign the words, but Matthew doesn't give her the chance.

He turns his back on her, on Hannah and Edgar too, and storms out of the kitchen, leaving only blood and silence in his wake. Olivia lashes out, swipes her arm across the table and sends the tin box of gauze and tape crashing to the floor. Matthew doesn't look back.

Tears burn behind her eyes, threatening to fall.

But she doesn't let them. When people see tears, they stop listening to your hands or your words or anything else you have to say. And it doesn't matter if the tears are angry or sad, frightened or frustrated. All they see is a girl crying.

So she holds them in as somewhere, deep inside the house, a door slams shut.

Hannah does not assure her.

Edgar does not say that it will pass.

They do not tell her to ignore her cousin, to get some rest, that it will all be better in the morning. Olivia has so many questions, but she can tell by the weight of the air, the horrible, held-breath stillness, that no one plans to answer them.

Hannah sinks into a chair, head bowed, hands disappearing into wild curls.

Edgar moves to comfort her, and Olivia goes upstairs to pack.

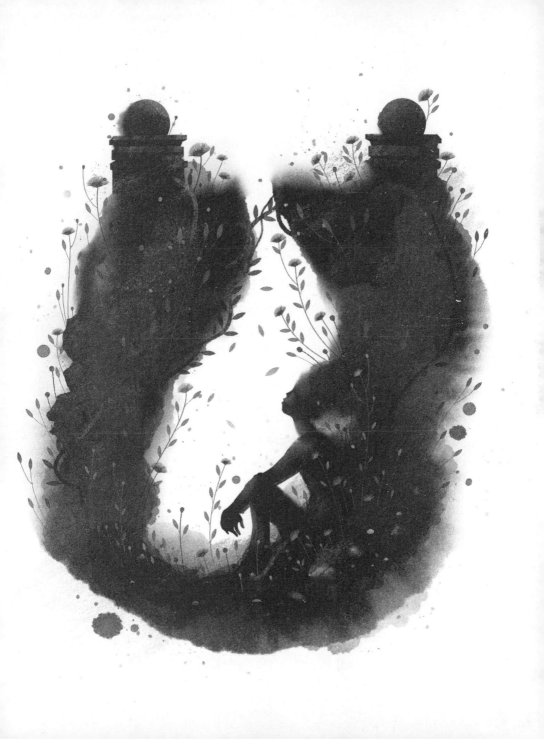

Chapter Twenty-One

Olivia moves through the house like a ghoul, feeling half-there, half-gone, dazed and sore and uncertain.

On the stairs she stops, remembering the eerie silver light that swept through the other house. In the hall, she sees the door to Matthew's room shut fast, the mottled shadow of moving feet beneath. Her uncle's ghoul stands guard outside and will not meet her gaze. In her mother's room, she turns the gold key in the lock, remembering the hum of iron under her hands, the door answering to blood. Hers and Matthew's. Prior blood.

There must always be a Prior at the gate.

With my blood, I seal this door.

Father calls it a prison.

And we the keepers.

I was born to die in this house.

What have you done?

Olivia's head spins.

She looks down at her bare feet, caked with mud and dust, the shallow red scrape of thorns that wrap around her calves, too tired, too shaken, to feel any of it. She passes the suitcase and the bed, walks straight into the tiled bathroom, and runs a bath, as hot as it will go.

As it fills, she stands before the bathroom mirror, studying her face, her eyes, her dress, all of her coated in ash and blood and things she cannot see but feel, the ghoul's hand on her mouth, the mouse twitching in her palm, the dead-white eyes hanging on her in the dark, and suddenly she wants to climb out of her clothes, out of her skin.

She strips away the stained blue dress and climbs down into the too-hot water, watching as it clouds. She works one-handed, scouring her skin, trying to scrub away the eerie chill, the dancers' ashes, the boy in the fountain she couldn't reach, the door that wouldn't open, and the fear of what would have happened if the soldiers had caught up with her. She tries to scrub away the other side of the wall, the terror she felt with every step, but also the eerie sense of coming home. As if some part of her belonged in that dead, decaying house.

And of course, it did.

She is her father's daughter, after all.

The tallest shadow.

She tries to imagine him as one of the dancers, turning like a puppet across the ballroom floor, but she knows in her bones he wasn't one of them.

Death, with his four shadows and his dozen shades.

Four shadows, and she counted only three, ranged around the throne.

The water clouds, and in the swirling surface she conjures another soldier, not broad or thin or short but tall, standing dark eyed and armor clad upon the platform. She sees him hunting her mother through the ruined house. Catching her. And setting her free.

Olivia studies her hands below the water, the heat causing pink to bloom across her skin. The gray film she washed away still hangs in the bath, wrapping like tendrils around her fingers. A mother made of flesh and blood. A father made of ash and bone.

What does that make *her*?

The water has gone cold and fogged with all the things she's washed away, and she climbs out and pulls the plug, watching it drain. Her mother's blue dress lies ruined on the tile, and she leaves it there, opens the suitcase she never unpacked and pulls on the second gray shift she brought, the fabric stiff and scratchy and ill-fitting. Only a matter of days, but she can hardly stand the feel of it now against her skin. She strips it off and pulls on a pale green dress instead.

And then, she packs.

Not because Matthew told her to, but because she longs to find a place where she is wanted. And she is not wanted here. She stares down at the pile of pale fabric in her suitcase, then flings open the wardrobe and pulls out her mother's clothes.

The case is too small, they'll never fit, but she doesn't care, she has lost enough and she is taking this. One by one the garments come free of their hangers, one by one they drop like flowers cut, until the wardrobe is empty, the floor strewn with cloth, and Olivia collapses, chest heaving, among the garden of her mother's dresses, the bright yellows and bold reds and hazy blues, like summer blooms.

Something cracks inside her, a soft, hitching breath.

The tears come then, bitter and hot.

She hates them even as they fall.

She has only cried twice, once when she was old enough to read the book and realize that for all her games and all the lies she told herself, her parents were never coming back. And once after Anabelle tore the pages out. Not when she heard the horrible rip, but later, after she'd risen up to fill the jar with bugs, after she'd dumped them in Anabelle's bed and crawled back into her own, she'd curled up in the dark and sobbed, the torn pages of the journal clutched against her chest.

Her mother's journal. She keeps flexing her fingers, desperate to feel the familiar weight of the book. But it's gone. Lost beyond the wall, and the grief hits her in a wave.

It is not the *words* she mourns—she has memorized them all—it is her father's drawings, the ones she'd only just begun to understand. It is the object itself, the indentation of the pen on the paper, the grooves in the cover, the letter in the back, *Olivia, Olivia, Olivia,* her name written over and over in her mother's hand.

The mother who fled this place.

Who warned her never to return.

The mother she misses, despite the fact she never knew her.

A slight draft slips through the room, though the window is shuttered and the door is closed.

And then the ghoul is there. There is less of it than the ones beyond the wall—half a shoulder is missing, part of a hip, an arm—but it is there, ankles crossed, leaning forward elbow balanced on one knee, chin resting on its palm.

Her vision blurred with tears, Olivia can almost imagine the woman on the bed is real. Perhaps she is. Real, she is learning, is a slippery thing, not a solid black line but a shape with soft edges, a great deal of gray.

She doesn't look up, afraid that the ghoul will disappear. She sits there, head bowed among her mother's dresses, even as she senses movement, even as she feels the ghoul rising from the bed and stepping forward into the pool of cotton and wool and silk, sinking to its knees in front of her. They would be nearly eye to eye if she looked up.

And she cannot help herself. She does.

When Olivia lifts her gaze, the ghoul flickers slightly, like a candle in the breeze, but then steadies. Perhaps it has never been the looking that banished ghouls. Perhaps it is the thinking, the pointed *go away* she's always lobbed at them as she glared.

Now Olivia stares at what's left of her mother.

What happened to you? she thinks.

It is not like Uncle Arthur, with his face half gone. There is no gunshot wound, no blade, no culprit, but the ghoul is painfully thin, and there are hollows beneath its eyes, and Olivia remembers the entries in the journal, the sleep her mother could not find, her fear of drowning in her dreams.

Tired can be a kind of sick, Edgar said, *if it lasts long enough.*

Whatever illness took her mother, it is taking Matthew too. And she doesn't know how to stop it, doesn't know how to keep it from coming for her next.

Why did you leave Gallant? she wants to ask.

Why did you leave me?

The ghoul's hand drifts up, and Olivia holds her breath, hoping it means to speak, to sign, but its fingers simply brush the air beside her face, as if to cup her cheek or tuck a strand behind her ear, and Olivia cannot help herself, she throws her arms around her mother's neck, desperate to be held.

But here, the ghouls aren't real enough to touch. Here, they are only fragile shadows of the dead, and her hands go straight through. She tumbles forward, landing among her mother's dresses. Pain lances through her wounded palm. And when she scrambles up again, she is alone.

Olivia sags, wishing, for the briefest moment, that she were back beyond the wall.

Gallant has gone quiet.

Not the eerie quiet of the other house, or the restful quiet of a place asleep, but the tense quiet of bodies retreating to their corners. Somewhere, Hannah is leaning into Edgar. Somewhere, Matthew lies awake and waits for dawn.

The windows are shut fast, and she knows that day won't break for another hour, at least. Matron Jessamine used to say this was the darkest part of the night, after the moon and before the sun.

Olivia hauls her small suitcase to the bottom of the stairs and leaves it there.

She pads barefoot through the empty halls, the way she did her first night here. Already, she has learned the layout of the sprawling house, and she finds her way without a candle past the row of portraits to the music room, her mother's red journal tucked beneath her arm.

The piano sits abandoned in the dark.

No Matthew. No moonlight. The garden nothing but a wall of textured black.

Olivia climbs into the bay window with the red journal. It is far too dark to read, but she doesn't plan to read. Instead she peels back the cover, turning past curling text until she finds the final entry. And then, turning once more, to the blank pages beyond.

There, she begins to write.

If you read this, I am safe.

Her father's drawings are lost, but her mother's words are safe, read a thousand times and pressed into the pages of her memory. And there, in the dark, her pencil hisses over the page as she resurrects each and every one.

> *I dreamed of you last night.*
> *If I gave you my hand, would you take it?*
> *What will we call her?*

And with every reconstructed line, she understands, Grace Prior wasn't mad. She was lonely and lost, wild and free, desperate and haunted.

And she did everything she could.

Even if it meant leaving her daughter.

Even if it meant letting her go.

There is so much she still doesn't understand, but that, at last, she knows.

Olivia writes until she reaches the last entry, scrawls the letter to herself in the back of the red book.

> *Olivia, Olivia, Olivia*
> *Remember this—*
> *the shadows are not real*
> *the dreams can never hurt you*
> *and you will be safe, as long as you stay away from Gallant.*

She stares at her mother's words in her own hand for a very long time and then closes the journal and presses it to her front.

Exhaustion curls over her like smoke, but she does not sleep.

Instead, she keeps her eyes on the window, on the garden, the thinnest trails of daylight winding through.

She will not go back to Merilance. The car may come to take her there, but it is a long road, and it will have to stop at least once, and when it does, she will leave. She will run away, as her mother did, as she always meant to do herself. Perhaps she will flee into a city, become a vagabond, a thief.

Perhaps she will go to the ocean, sneak aboard a ship, and sail away.

Perhaps she will slip into that quiet little town and work in the pasty shop, and be a mystery to everyone who comes and goes, and she will grow up and grow old, and no one will ever know she was an orphan who saw ghouls and once met Death and lived in a house beside a wall.

The master of the house is angry.

He makes his way to the garden wall, a pair of yellow boots hanging from one hand like just-plucked fruit.

The shadows stand there, waiting.

"You let her get away," he says in a voice like frost.

Their heads droop as one, eyes on the barren ground, and he wonders what excuses they would give if they could speak. He studies the door, where two small palms have struck again and again, knocking away the crust of long-dead leaves, exposing the iron beneath.

He runs a hand thoughtfully over the stain, then turns and makes his way back up the garden path. The dead roses lean away, but a single, bursting bloom hangs across his path, the petals full and heavy.

The master of the house traces the life back down its leaves, its stem, its roots.

"Very good," he says, plucking the flower.

And then he smiles, a small, wicked smile, a smile the moonlight doesn't land on, a smile just between the garden and his teeth.

Part Five
BLOOD AND IRON

Chapter Twenty-Two

Rain drums its fingers on the garden shed.

The ghoul stares out from the corner.

Olivia shifts her weight, feels something crack under her shoe. She looks down, expecting to find one of the many clay pot shards littering the ground, but the piece is porcelain, roses and thorns curling over a white ground, and she knows it belongs to a vase, though she isn't sure how. The ghoul holds a half-formed finger to the empty space where its lips should be. The rain has stopped, and Olivia knows she better be getting back, if she's going to go, but when she steps outside, there is no gray gravel moat, no grim stone building, no Merilance.

Instead, she's in the garden at Gallant. A riot of color blooms to every side, and of course she is here—how could she forget?

She turns toward the garden wall and sees her mother standing there by the gate, in a yellow sundress, in the shadow of the stone, one hand lifting to the iron door. Olivia opens her mouth, wishing she could call out, but she can't, of course, so she runs.

Flings herself down the garden path, hoping to catch her mother before she opens the gate, but just as the woman at the wall turns to look over her shoulder, Olivia stumbles and falls. Lands hard on the ground, which isn't grassy and soft but a tangle of brittle ivy over dead earth. She scrambles up again, but it's dark, and she's on the wrong side of the wall.

The house that isn't Gallant rises like a broken tooth, and she twists back to the gate and sees her mother standing in the open door, a tall shadow at her side. Olivia stumbles toward her parents but as she gets closer, she realizes the shadow isn't her father. It's the man who isn't a man, the master of the other house, bone jaw shining through his torn cheek as he smiles and slams the door shut, and Olivia wakes up.

She gasps, the red journal falling to the floor. She blinks, one hand raised against the sunlight spilling in through the bay window, cloud-white and bright. It is far past dawn, hardly still morning. Her head is thick, her hand throbbing dully. Someone has laid a blanket over her, and when she looks up, she finds she is not alone.

Matthew sits on the edge of the piano bench, head bowed, picking at the bandage on his own palm. They make strange mirrors, each with a hand wrapped in linen, his clean and hers stained.

When she straightens, so does he. Their gazes meet, and she braces for an assault. But he just looks at her with those tired, haunted eyes, and says, "You're awake."

Again, not a question. Never a question. Matthew's sentences always seem to end in periods. She nods once, curtly, expects that the car is waiting, and he has come to rouse her and send her on her way. She pictures Hannah and Edgar in the foyer, her suitcase already loaded in the car. But Matthew doesn't stand. He lets out a long, low breath and says, "I was angry."

Olivia waits, wondering if that is meant to be an apology. He swallows hard.

"I do not want you here," he mutters, and she lifts a brow, as if to say, I couldn't tell. But he is no longer looking at her; his gaze has drifted past her to the window and the garden and the wall. "But you deserve to know why."

He stands then, already turning toward the door. "Follow me."

And Olivia does. She takes up the fallen journal and trails him out of the music room.

"I should have told you about the wall," he says, "but I was afraid, if I did, you would go looking. I guess I hoped, if you left soon enough, it might not know that you were here. It might not find you." He glances back over his shoulder. "But then you went and found it anyway."

They walk down the hall of portraits, Matthew's gaze flicking for just a second to the patch of bare wall where one has been removed. His steps are slow, his breath audible, as if his body is working too hard just to carry itself along. She can hear Hannah and Edgar chatting in the kitchen—surely they don't mean to let her go without so much as a goodbye?

Matthew leads her past the ballroom, and she understands then where they are going.

The study door swings open, and Olivia follows him inside. For the briefest moment, she is back beyond the wall, in the other study, shoving the chair under the door as the wolf-like soldier barrels toward her.

But then she blinks, and the chair is in its place, and the shelves are lined with books, the wallpaper smooth, the sculpture waiting on the old wood desk. Her eyes flick to the far wall, wondering about the secret door as Matthew sinks into the chair behind the desk, as if the short trek across the house has stolen all his strength.

"It's not your fault you are a Prior," he says, "and Hannah is right, I cannot make you leave." Olivia's heart thrums, spirits rising, until he says, "But once you know the truth, you'll understand why you should."

He runs his hands through the thicket of his light brown hair and rests his chin on his folded arms and stares at the metal sculpture on the desk, his cheeks hollow and his eyes fever bright.

"So I'll tell you the story, as it was told to me."

He reaches out and rests one finger on the metal sculpture, giving it the slightest push. The whole thing tips into motion.

"Everything casts a shadow," he begins. "Even the world we

live in. And as with every shadow, there is a place where it must touch. A seam, where the shadow meets its source."

Olivia's heart quickens.

The wall.

"The wall," echoes Matthew. "The world you saw beyond the wall is a shadow of this one. But unlike most shadows, it isn't empty."

His gaze flicks up.

"Did you see it?"

She knows, without asking, that he means the gruesome figure in the other house, the master made of rot and ruin. Milk-white eyes and coal-black coat and jawbone shining through its tattered cheek.

Olivia nods, and Matthew swallows and goes on.

"Perhaps it began as nothing. A weed poking up through barren soil. Or perhaps it was always what it is—a destructive force—it doesn't matter. At some point, the thing in the dark grew hungry. It realized that it was living in the shadow of the world. And it wanted out."

Matthew keeps his gaze on the sculpture as he speaks, and Olivia too finds herself drawn to the revolving houses, the rhythm of them as they turn away and come together.

"Some people are repelled by darkness. Others are drawn to it, to the static crackle of power in a place. To the hum of magic, or the presence of the dead. They can see these forces staining the world like ink in water. Our family was like that. I told you Gallant wasn't built by Priors. The house was already here. Empty and waiting. And the Priors came. They felt called to the house, and when they arrived, they saw the wall for what it was—a threshold. A line between."

Matthew's voice is low and steady. He knows these words the way she knows her mother's.

"By day, the wall was just a wall. But at night, when the lines between shadow and source grew thin enough, it became a gate. A way from one world into the other. And the thing in the dark began to *press* against the stones. The center of the wall began to split and crumble, and the Priors knew that soon enough, the thing in the dark would force its way out.

"So they forged an iron door and mounted it over the cracking stone, to keep the darkness back. And for a while, it was enough. And then it wasn't.

"One night, it escaped. The stone broke, and the iron fell, and it simply stepped into this world. Everywhere it walked, things died. It fed on every living thing, every blade of grass, every flower and tree and bird, leaving only dust and bones in its wake. It would have eaten everything."

Matthew drags a finger along the turning sculpture until it slows and slows and stops.

"The Priors all fought, but they were still flesh and blood and it was a demon, stealing every life it touched. They couldn't win. But they managed not to lose. They forced the creature back beyond the wall. Half the Priors held it there, and the others put the door back up. And this time, they soaked it edge to edge in their blood and swore that nothing would ever cross that gate without their blessing."

Olivia looks down at her bandaged hand, remembering her cousin's rage when she first cut herself. The way her skin split open as she pounded on the door, desperate to get free. Matthew's bleeding palm as he pressed it to the iron and sealed it shut again.

He guides the model on its arc until the two houses face one another. As they come to rest, the metal rings align between them.

"It is still there, the thing beyond the wall, still trying to get out. It's fighting now, harder than ever, not because it's strong, but because it's weak. It's running out of time. Out of *us*. There must always be a Prior at the gate. That is what my father said. And his father, and his, and his. But they were *wrong*."

Matthew lifts his head, and there is a defiant gleam in the dark of his eyes.

"It will not end until there are no Priors left. Don't you see? *Anyone* can guard the wall. Mend the cracks. Keep it standing. But *we* are the keys to that prison. Only *our* blood can open the door, and that *thing* in the dark will do anything to get it from us. It will torture us, turn every dream to nightmare, bend our minds until we break or—"

He grits his teeth, and she sees his father on his knees in the grass, the gun lifting to his temple.

"As long as there is a Prior in this house, it has a chance. That is why you should never have come. It is strongest here, beside the wall. If you go far enough, perhaps it will not find you."

Olivia swallows. Could that be true? No, it is a chance, perhaps, but not a promise. Her mother left, and still the darkness found her. And she is a Prior after all. Matthew may want to be the last, but he is not alone.

She shakes her head.

Matthew's fist hits the table, the force sending the metal rings back into motion.

"You have to go!" he shouts, but she doesn't. She won't.

He folds forward, lank curls shadowing his face, and she sees something drip onto the desk. Tears. "It cannot be for nothing," he says, throat tight. "I am so tired. I can't—" His voice breaks.

Olivia goes to her cousin, reaches out a cautious hand, expecting him to pull away. But he doesn't. Something in him breaks, and then the words spill out.

"It took my brother first."

Olivia pulls her hand back as if burned.

"It was two years ago," he says. "The darkness had never come for children. It always went for the older Priors. It was easier to get inside their heads. But it didn't come for my father. It didn't come for me. It came for Thomas. It drew him barefoot out of bed one night."

That is why they strap him down, she thinks. That is why his wrists are bruised and his eyes are dark.

"He was still asleep when it led him through the house and across the garden and around the wall. He was only twelve."

Her mind spins as she thinks of the boy she saw on the other side, the one curled at the bottom of the fountain. How old was he? His hair and skin looked faded, gray, but perhaps it was only a trick of the light, perhaps—

"I went after him, of course," says Matthew. "I had to. He'd always been afraid of the dark." His voice wavers, almost breaks. But he presses on. "My father wanted to go, but I said it should be me. I told him I was stronger, but the truth is, I simply couldn't bear the thought of losing them both." The breath catches in his throat. "So I went. And I saw the house beyond the wall. But I never went in. I didn't have to. The door on the other side was soaked with blood. There was so much of it. Too much. Someone had painted the door with my brother's life. Covered every iron inch." He tugs at the bandage on his palm.

"But that *thing* slaughtered my brother for nothing. Only a Prior's blood can open the door, but it has to be willingly given. Now it knows, and every night, I dream that he is still alive, still there on the other side of that godforsaken wall, calling out, pleading to be rescued and—what are you doing?"

Olivia has rounded the desk. She pushes him aside and pulls open the drawer, searching for a pen, even though she knows there isn't one, nothing but the little black book filled with places she might be. She pushes off the desk and plunges past Matthew out of the study and into the hall, hurrying toward the foyer, to her suitcase, because she knows, she knows, that she has seen him.

She kneels and throws it open, dragging out her sketchbook and her pencil. Doesn't even bother standing, just crouches there on the foyer's patterned floor and starts to draw.

Matthew's footsteps sound nearby, and then he's there, bracing himself against the banister as her pencil hisses over parchment, carving out a scene.

A boy, lying at the bottom of an empty fountain, bound to the feet of a broken statue. Folded in as if sleeping, his face half-hidden by curls.

She shoves the sketchpad into Matthew's hand, tapping it with the butt of the pencil.

"I don't understand," he says, looking from the paper to her and back. "What is this? Where did you . . ."

Olivia lets out an exasperated breath, wishing people would stop and *think* sometimes, fill in the words so she doesn't have to. She takes the sketchpad from him and turns back to the drawing she did of the wall. And it seems impossible for Matthew to get paler, but he does.

And then he grabs her wrist and pulls her up the stairs and down the hall, to the room she has only seen once, in the dead of night, when the screams drew her to the door. His bed is made now, the covers smoothed, his nightmares erased, at least from the sheets. But the cuffs peek out from under the bed, and he absently rubs one wrist, the bruises still bright against his too-pale skin.

Matthew goes to the far wall, the shape propped against it, covered by a white sheet. He pulls it back, revealing a picture frame. A family portrait.

The one missing from the downstairs hall. In it, her uncle stands in the garden, stern-faced but human and whole, one arm wrapped around his wife, Isabelle, holding her close. And there, before them, a pair of boys seated on a stone bench. Matthew, thirteen maybe, already long and lean, tawny hair swept half across his face. And a smaller boy, looking up at him with adoration.

"Is that who you saw?" asks Matthew, his words tight and small, as if they're caught inside his chest.

Olivia sinks to her knees before the portrait, studying Thomas Prior, laying this image over the one in her mind. He is younger than the boy she found in the fountain, but not by much. Here his eyes are bright and wide, there they were closed; here his curls look light brown instead of gray. But everything is gray beyond the wall. And there is no denying the slope of his cheek. The line of his nose. The angle of his chin.

"Is that him?" presses Matthew.

Olivia swallows and nods, and her cousin folds into the nearest chair, his bandaged hand pressed to his mouth.

"It's been two years," he says, and she doesn't know if he's thinking that the boy in the fountain can't be his brother, or about how long he left him there. How long he thought him dead.

All the movement in the halls has drawn Hannah. She stands in the doorway, uncertain.

"What's going on?" she asks.

Matthew looks up. "It's Thomas," he says, eyes bright with fear and hope. "He's still alive."

Chapter Twenty-Three

"I have to find my brother," he demands. "I have to bring him home."

They are standing in the kitchen, the only four people in the too-large house. Edgar scrubs the garden from his hands, and Hannah twists a kitchen towel between her fingers, and Matthew paces, the color high in his cheeks, and Olivia wonders if she's made a terrible mistake.

Back at Merilance, she learned about *life*. The way it started, and the way it ended. It was always talked about as a one-way street, first alive and then dead, and even though she knew it was more complicated—because of the ghouls, who had clearly been alive, and then dead, and now were something else—the truth is, she isn't sure what to make of the boy in the fountain.

She doesn't *think* the boy was dead, but she also didn't see the rise and fall of his chest, the subtle stirrings of a body just asleep. If it is a spell, she hopes it's one that she can break. Hopes that she will touch his hand and he will wake.

Then there is the fact of time. It's been two years. He should be fourteen, but the shape on the cracked stone floor was still a child. Then again, nothing seems to grow beyond the wall. Perhaps it is the same for people.

"Is it even possible?" asks Hannah, busying her hands with a pot of soup no one intends to eat. Olivia has told the story now, of her trip beyond the wall, or at least of finding the boy, and Edgar has done his best to translate, his brows knitting more with every word.

He clears his throat. "I hate to say it, but it could be a trap."

As if that isn't obvious. *Of course* it is a trap. A stolen child, left out like bait. But traps are like locks. They can be picked. They can be opened. A trap is only a trap if you get caught. Olivia knows better now, and when she goes back—

"I'll go tonight," says Matthew.

"No," say Hannah and Edgar and Olivia at the same time, two out loud, and one with a single cutting swipe.

"He's my brother," persists Matthew. "I left him once. I will not be the one to leave again."

Olivia lets out a short breath. And then she walks up to her cousin and pushes him once, hard. Matthew staggers back into the counter, looking more shocked than hurt, but she has made her point. He can barely stand. The color in his cheeks is not health, but sickness. He is worn thin, hollowed out by lack of sleep, and she has been beyond the wall and back again. She has seen what lurks in the shadows, what lives in the dark.

She looks from Matthew to Edgar to Hannah.

She doesn't know how to tell them about the ghouls, the way they rise to meet her when she calls. She makes no mention of the life that stirs beneath her fingers there, sudden and wild. She doesn't say that she is her father's daughter, too, that some part of her *belongs* beyond that wall. That if anyone can cross into a world of death and come out alive again, it's her.

Matthew's hand clenches into a fist against the counter. "He's my brother," he says again, a pleading in his voice. Olivia nods and takes his bandaged hand in hers.

I know, she says with a look, the subtle squeeze of her fingers. *And I will bring him back.*

They have six hours until dusk.

Too much time, and not enough.

Hannah thinks she should eat, and Edgar thinks she should rest, and Matthew thinks he should be doing this instead. Olivia cannot eat or rest or hand the burden over. All she can do is prepare—and the more she knows about the workings of this place, the better. She has spent the last few days learning the layout of the halls, but now she looks around, at the walls and the floors, and wonders.

The world you saw beyond the wall is a shadow of this one.

Matthew's words turn inside her head, like the houses in their metal frame. The houses, Gallant and not Gallant, one soft and frayed, the other in a state of disrepair, but otherwise, they are the same.

Olivia returns to the study, her cousin on her heels.

She goes to the wall behind the desk, to the place where shelf meets paper.

"What are you doing?" he asks as she runs her hand over the wall, trying to find the seam. It was there in the other house, and so—

Her fingers find a groove in the papered wall. She presses her palm flat, and the hidden door gives, just a little, before swinging open onto a narrow corridor. She knows if she follows it, she will find herself standing in the kitchen.

Matthew stares at her as if she's just performed a magic trick.

"How did you know . . ." he begins, and she doesn't have the time to tell him, to draw the ghoul, its hand over her mouth, so she goes to the model with its two miniature houses, its concentric metal rings. She points first at one house and then the other, drawing an invisible line between the two.

Matthew's eyes narrow and then brighten.

"What's there is here," he muses, and she nods and turns to the drawing she did in the garden, the one of Gallant itself, taps the pencil expectantly as if to say, Where else? Understanding blooms across his face.

"Follow me."

Every house has secrets.

Merilance had no hidden tunnels or false walls, but it did have a loose floorboard in the hall, a nook just wide enough to hide in at the top of the north stairs, a dozen cracks and shadows to exploit. Gallant's secrets are far greater.

Olivia learns them now, presses each into her mind like a wildflower between the pages of her sketchpad.

There is the passage she's already found, the lightless tunnel that runs between the study and the kitchen. Matthew shows her another. He leads her to the ballroom, to the wooden molding that runs along the far wall, as high as her waist. She watches him feel along the wood until he finds the notch.

"Here," he says, taking her fingers and guiding them to the trim. It feels like a chip, broken away, but when she presses down, the wooden panel swings out, revealing a cubby too small for all but a child—or a narrow girl. She crouches down, squinting into the dark, until Matthew lifts a lamp, and by it, she can see a set of squat stone steps.

"It leads down into the cellar," he explains.

The cellar. She has only seen it once, the morning after she arrived, when Hannah emerged with the basket on her hip. But she can think of a hundred places she'd rather go than the dry-stone crypt beneath the house. Still, as she eases the door shut, she forces herself to note the chip in the wood, how far it is from the corner, until she's sure she could find it in the dark.

They are not alone on their quest. As Matthew leads her through the house, she sees them, watching. A ghoul in the corner. Another on the stairs. Half-formed faces she knows from the paintings in the hall outside the study. Members of a family she never knew she had. Priors, just like the ghouls beyond the wall, the ones who never made it home.

She follows Matthew into the music room next. Her fingers itch, wishing they could simply sit and play, wishing he would teach her another song. But he doesn't stop at the piano. He goes past it, to the right corner of the room, finds the groove where two strips of wallpaper seem to meet.

"Right here," he says, pressing his hand flat to the wood. And for a moment, she expects him to command the hidden door, to order it open or closed the way he did the garden gate. But there is no blood on his palm, and he gives no order, simply presses down, and a panel pops out.

"Come on," he says, gesturing for her to follow.

The stairs are so steep and narrow, they are nearly a ladder. He leads the way up and at the top, they step out into Matthew's room.

He sinks onto the edge of his bed to catch his breath.

"My brother made a game of it," he says, "finding all the secret places." And though he's hiding it well, she can see the weariness sweeping through his face, the faint tremor in his hands.

He gestures at the wall across from the bed, at a garden tapestry that hangs there. When she draws it back, she finds a door. Not a hidden one, folded straight into the molding or the wood, but an ordinary door, the tapestry obviously added to put it out of sight.

A small gold key hangs from the lock, and Olivia looks to Matthew for permission. He nods once, and she turns the key. It whispers in the lock, and the door opens, not onto a bathroom or a hall, but another bedroom, a little smaller than his own.

The shutters are open, the curtains pulled back, the late afternoon light spilling in over a desk, a chest, a bed. A tattered bear propped on the pillow, a pair of shoes nestled neatly by the bedside table. Thomas's room.

She pictures Hannah coming in here every morning. Edgar latching the shutters every night. They may go through the motions, but the room still feels abandoned. The floorboards too stiff, the dust that hangs in the air, even after being swept from every surface.

Olivia returns to Matthew's room and closes the door, turning the little gold key in the lock. He sighs and rises from the bed. And as she follows him out, down the main stairs, she thinks of all the halls and all the rooms and all the hidden doors in Gallant. Perhaps she won't need any of them. Perhaps the boy will still be there, in the fountain's empty bowl, and she will never set foot again inside the other house. Perhaps it will be that easy—but she doubts it.

Three hours until dusk. Matthew is resting, but Olivia's skin hums with nerves, and she goes out into the garden to get some air. The day is warm, and she walks between the flowers, eyes trailing over pink and gold and green before she sees it at the garden's edge.

One of the roses has died in the night, as if a sudden frost stole in. The stem looks brittle, the leaves have curled, the head droops. A sharp slice of winter in the summer yard. As she nears it, she sees the gray weed wrapped like a hand around the rose's throat.

Olivia's fingers twitch, the memory of the other garden, the way dead flowers surged to life against her palm. She reaches out with her good hand, questing, careful, as if the rose is made of glass and just as sharp. Slowly, she cups a withered bloom, paper dry against her skin, and waits to feel the prickle, the chill, as she breathes life back into the flower.

But nothing happens.

Olivia frowns, tightening her grip, trying to force energy into the rose. But the flower only cracks and crumbles as the petals tumble free, scattering across the lawn. She looks down at her fingers, the dust of the dead rose a shadow on her hand.

Whatever power she might have beyond the wall, she does not have it here.

Two hours until dusk.

Her suitcase has vanished from the foyer, returned to the foot of her bed. Olivia changes out of her mother's pink dress, climbing into her own gray shift, knowing it will blend into the world beyond the wall. She holds her breath as she does up the buttons, as if the clothes are a kind of spell, as if she might fade back into the girl she was at Merilance.

But she doesn't. She can't. She has never been a Merilance girl.

In the bathroom, she studies her reflection, her charcoal hair, her slate-gray eyes, her sallow skin. She looks like something from beyond the wall. Pictures herself silver lit inside the other house, twirling across the ballroom floor. A snap of thin fingers, and she is ash.

But then she sees her mother's comb on the counter, the flowers summer blue. Imagines Grace Prior at her back, touching her shoulders, leaning in to whisper that it will be all right, that home is a choice, that she belongs here as much as there.

She takes up the flower comb, tucks it in her hair.

Beyond the window, the light is going thin. She looks down at the stone fountain, the woman with the outstretched hand, and she knows now it is a warning. *Stay back*, it says. But it is a message meant for strangers. She is a Prior, and Gallant is her house.

One hour until dusk, and every minute seems to drag. Olivia cannot stand the wait, wants to plunge back into that other world, to fling herself across the wall, but as long as the sun is up, the wall is nothing more than what it seems. All she can do is wait.

Wait and hope that she finds Thomas.

Wait and hope that Death does not find her.

Wait and hope that this will work.

And then what?

The question tangles through her like a weed.

Matthew said the thing beyond the wall is hungry, that it will never stop. But he also said that it is dying, that he meant to starve it out. Could they outlast its final, desperate throes, or will it only end when they do? If she stays, could they be a kind of family? Or will she have to watch her cousin waste away and wait for the dreams to turn on her as well?

A shadow crosses the doorway. Matthew stands there, waiting. He looks past her to the window, where day has turned to dusk, and says what she already knows.

"It's time."

Chapter Twenty-Four

Downstairs, Hannah is latching the shutters.

Edgar is locking the doors.

And Matthew is lecturing them all. Perhaps it is only hope, but his back is straight and his gaze is focused, and Olivia can imagine the boy he might have been once, the man he could become, if the thing beyond the wall had not stolen his family, if the darkness had not frayed his nerves, and the nightmares had not whittled him so thin.

It is a simple enough plan, but he goes over it again.

Olivia will find Thomas and return to the wall. Matthew will be waiting on the Gallant side to let them out. She will knock three times, and he will open the door and seal it again in their wake before anything else can get through.

She imagines Matthew standing at the gate, palms pressed against the iron to feel the knocks, imagines the darkness whispering through his head, trying to coax him to unlock the door, to step through and see for himself. She wonders if he will hear his brother's voice. At least he will not hear hers.

"You have to get back to the door," he says, and the set of his jaw, the steel in his gaze, tells her if she fails, if she is caught, he will not come. He will leave her there beyond the wall.

As for Edgar and Hannah—

"You must not leave the house," he warns them.

"And if something gets past you?" asks Hannah. "What then?"

"Go down into the cellar."

Edgar snorts, a shotgun resting on his shoulder. "I think not."

"You have to hide."

"We may be old, but we have fight left in us."

"Who are you calling old?" snipes Hannah, taking up a fire poker.

"You are not Priors," says Matthew grimly. "You have nothing it wants. Nothing to give, and everything to lose."

"This is our house as much as yours, Matthew Prior," says Hannah. "And we will defend it."

"You will *die*."

Edgar stands his ground. "Death comes for everything."

Olivia stares at them, these people she is just beginning to know, this makeshift family, but all she sees are the dancers in the ballroom, the way they turned to ash.

It will not come to that, she tells herself as she flexes her fingers, the bandage tight over her palm. Her hands are empty, the sketchpad and the red journal left on her bed. She wishes she had something to hold. A hand. Or a knife. She sighs, fingers dropping to her side.

But as she takes in Hannah's curls, threaded gray, Edgar's stooping shoulders, Matthew, already winded—she bites back a silent laugh. Not the laugh you make when you're amused, but the one that escapes when you know you're in trouble.

Hannah pulls her into a tight hug, one that seems to wrap all the way around her like a coat. Olivia wishes they could stay like that forever.

"Just a child," the woman murmurs, half to herself, and Olivia can feel a teardrop hitting her hair and knows Hannah is thinking of Thomas as much as her, and maybe even of her mother, and her uncle, of every Prior she's met and known and lost beyond the wall.

Hannah cups Olivia's cheek, tipping her chin so their eyes meet. "You come back," she says. "Thomas or no, you come back."

Olivia nods.

And then Matthew is leading her out into the garden. Away from one house and toward another. She looks back at Gallant, one last time—at Hannah and Edgar watching from the music room, little more than outlines in the failing light. At the ghouls that gather, the old one at the edge of the orchard, her uncle at the back door, a woman beneath a trellis, her mother sitting on a low stone bench. None of them tries to stop her as she and Matthew make their way to the wall.

But as they near it, she slows.

There is a new shadow on the ground. It fans out, the way lamplight does when it falls through an open door, though the one in the wall is closed.

Olivia kneels to study the mark.

It fed on every living thing, every blade of grass, every flower and tree and bird, leaving only dust and bones in its wake.

How do you fight something like that? she wonders and hopes she does not have to.

She runs her fingers over the grass. It's dry and brittle and black.

The door was only open a second, maybe two, and in that time, the other side burned its way into this one. What would it have done in an hour? A day?

It would have eaten everything.

She looks down at her own hand where it rests on the barren earth.

The *thing* beyond the wall can strip life from this world, but in that world she can give it back. Is that a weapon, or a weakness? She doesn't know.

Olivia straightens and finds Matthew staring at the door.

"Are you certain?" he asks. And she knows he must look at her and see a foolish, headstrong girl, a strange intruder on his stranger world, or worse, someone else to lose. He does not know what she can do. Then again, neither does she.

He looks at her and asks again, "Are you certain?" and she nods, not because she is, but because it is the only answer she can give. The only one that will keep Matthew alive, and bring his brother home.

Night is sweeping in now, and she turns to make her way to the edge of the wall, only to feel Matthew catch her wrist and pull her back. She tenses on instinct, unsure whether he means to quarrel or drag her into a hug.

He does neither. He simply rests his hands on her shoulders and looks her in the eyes.

"I will be right here," he says. "When you come back."

All her life, Olivia has wondered what it would feel like to have a family.

And now she knows.

It feels like this.

Olivia nods and squeezes her cousin's hand.

And then she takes a deep breath and steps around the wall.

For a moment, nothing happens.

She is back in the empty field, the sea of tallgrass rippling in the breeze, a few weedy thistles jutting here and there between the stems. The mountains rise, craggy old stone peaks so far away they look painted on the sky, and she can feel the wall behind her, and the world beyond it, the warmth of the garden at her back.

There is still time to turn around.

Perhaps seconds, perhaps heartbeats, but there is still time. Olivia closes her eyes and holds her ground. Between one breath and the next, the world settles. She feels it the way you feel a cloud as it passes overhead, blotting out the sun. When she opens her eyes, the field is gone, and she is back in the wasted garden, staring up at the ruined old house.

No figure stands on the balcony. No milk-white eyes shine in the dark. Still, her hand drifts to the pocket of her dress, to the hunting knife hidden there, a short, heavy blade in a leather sheath. Edgar pressed it into her hands just before she left.

"Pointy end out," he said, patting her shoulder, and she wanted to tell him she knew how to use a knife, even if the only thing she's ever cut are carrots and potatoes.

She doesn't draw the blade, isn't sure what good it will do against the monster in the dark, but it is enough to know that it is there.

Go, hisses a voice in her head, and she forces her legs forward, up the slope into the garden, moving like a thief.

Once, back at Merilance, she nearly got caught.

She was in Matron Agatha's room, kneeling in front of the bedside drawer, searching the contents more out of boredom than need, when the doorknob turned and the old woman came in, her shuffling steps and stale perfume filling the narrow space.

There was no room to hide beneath the bed, cluttered as it was, and if the matron had turned on the light, she would have seen Olivia there, but she didn't. She stumbled, sighing, through the darkened room and sank onto the bed, eyes glassy with Matron Sarah's sherry. She just sat there, staring at nothing, and Olivia knew she could either kneel there all night, waiting for the old woman to drift off, or make her escape, and in the end she decided she'd rather be caught fleeing than stay trapped, so she went.

Only she didn't break for the door, didn't run.

Instead, she held her breath and moved through the dark, slow as a shadow sliding over the wooden floor. And Agatha never even noticed.

That is how she moves through the garden now.

She passes the roses she touched the night before. Surrounded by dead limbs, that single plant blooms, petals blue-black beneath a blanket of silver light. Something sings beneath her skin at the sight of it, the urge to reach out again, to run her hands over the other wilted things. How many could she revive? It hurt, a little, that prickle, that chill, but it was wondrous, too. How let down she'd been in the other garden, when nothing rose to meet her touch.

Go on, says a voice in her head, but there is something strange about it, as if the thought is not quite hers. She forces her hands into fists and keeps walking.

Ahead, the house draws her eye like a candle in the dark, like a ghoul in the corner of a garden shed, and she has to stifle the urge to look, keeping her attention instead on the tangled stretch that curls around the side of the estate.

In the dark, the dead limbs and twisted husks make shadows everywhere. Nothing moves, and everything seems to move at once. The ground is uneven, old roots pushing up, thorny weeds sprawling, as if they'd had one last, riotous bloom, spilling over their banks before losing their hold on life. It would be so easy to snag on a sharp branch or fall, and she is sure that if she cuts herself, the ground will know. The thing in the house will know. If it does not already.

So Olivia steps carefully, trying to summon a patience she has never had as she moves in the shadow of the house that is not Gallant, to the front drive.

And the fountain.

No moon, but silver light still falls on the statue rising at its center.

The woman looms, dress chipped and arm broken, the basin hidden from view.

Olivia draws Edgar's knife and scans the drive, so exposed compared to the garden. No cover, nothing but the bare stretch of gravel. Her eyes flick to the front steps. Empty. The front doors. Closed. No sign of the three soldiers in their glinting armor.

No sense in waiting. She darts forward, the gravel shouting under her shoes, too loud, too loud, as she races to the fountain, hoping to reach the stone lip and see Thomas curled in the bottom, and—

The fountain is empty.

Nothing but cracked stone and several threads of ivy, the same ivy that was wrapped around his wrists, now broken and cast off on the basin floor.

Olivia hisses through her teeth. She knew it wouldn't be that easy.

She turns, expecting an ambush.

But all around her, the grounds are still.

The shadows do not move.

She puts away the knife, takes a step toward the house beyond the wall. Then stops.

There's a difference, after all, between walking into a trap and slipping between its teeth, storming through and skirting the edges. She creeps to the door on the side of the house, the one that leads in to the kitchen. Hovers, breath held, listening for sounds of life or motion.

The door whispers open, but in the heavy silence of this place, the whisper might as well be a whistle.

Olivia jumps back, pressing herself into the cool stone side of the house. She waits for the sound of boots, waits for the soldiers, for the master of the house. She waits until the silence settles like a sheet, until the world falls still around her. And then she steels herself and steps inside.

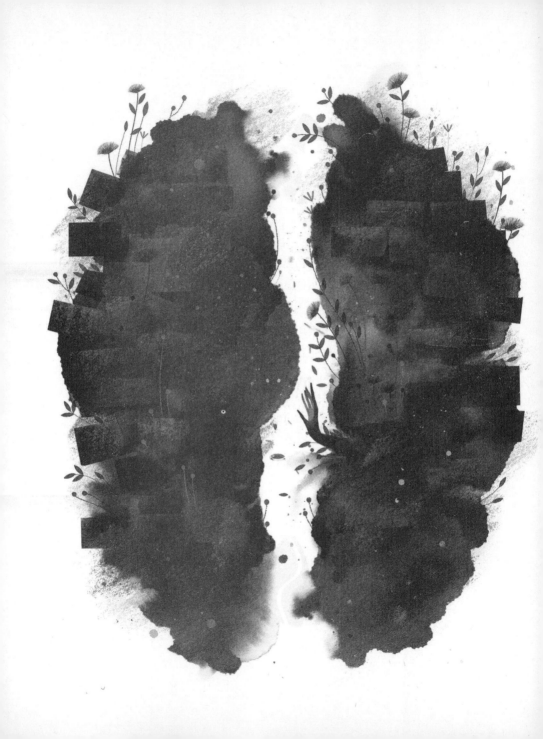

Chapter Twenty-Five

Olivia tells herself it is a game.

Like hide and seek. Like tag. The kinds of games the girls played back at Merilance, after the lights went out. Games Olivia always watched, but was never called to join, because she was too good at hiding, because she was no fun to find, since she never yelped or laughed or screamed.

It is just a game, she thinks as she creeps through the kitchen. The floor tiles are cracked and broken, but she does her best to move with quick and silent steps, past the empty cabinets and the barren shelves, the apple still sitting, shrunken, on the counter. She peers into the darkened hall.

Where are you? she wonders, trying to keep her thoughts as quiet as her feet.

Something moves behind her, and she spins, heart lunging up into her throat. But it's just a ghoul. The ruined echo of a young man, details drawing together and crumbling apart. She sees the slope of its shoulders, and the shape of its eyes, deep-set and dark in that familiar way.

The Priors all fought . . . they forced the creature back beyond the wall. . . .

And they never came home. The door was sealed. Their lives, a forfeit in the fight. The ghouls here, all Priors who died to keep the darkness in its cage.

Olivia begins to sign, then stops, remembering there is no need.

The ghouls can hear her.

Where is the boy? she asks, waiting for the ghoul to gesture to a room, a door, to show her which way to go. But it only shakes its head, and there is something in the rapid side to side, not a refusal so much as a plea.

Do not look, it seems to say.

But Olivia has no choice.

Answer me, she thinks, trying to make the thought an order. *Where is Thomas Prior?*

But the ghoul will not say. It shakes its head again, hand drawing through the air.

You must go.

But she can't. She can't go back without the boy. She can't see the look on Matthew's face. Can't let her family down.

She leaves the kitchen and the ghoul behind, stepping through into the hall. The floorboards warp and sag and splinter. The air tastes like dust. The hall branches, some doors open, and others closed. The house is too large. He could be anywhere.

For a moment she has a mad idea.

She closes her eyes, imagines herself a part of this place, and tries to reach out and feel him, as if he were a patch of sun, a pulse. They are connected after all, two Priors, two living bodies in a house full of ash. So she reaches, and hopes, and feels . . .

Nothing. Just foolish.

Wherever Thomas is, she will have to find him the old-fashioned way. By looking. So she moves through the house, torn between keeping to the shadows, which might not be empty, and walking through the moonlit halls, alone, exposed.

She passes the ballroom, but tonight there are no dancers spinning silently across the floor, no soldiers ranged about, no white-eyed figure on his makeshift throne.

The study door hangs open, listing on its broken hinges, the chair turned away behind the desk. She holds her breath as she creeps forward, waiting to hear that eerie voice from the other side, waiting for the chair to turn and reveal those dead-white eyes, that paper skin, bone jaw shining through its face. But she reaches the chair, and it is empty.

Olivia lets out a slow, unsteady sigh, heart racing in her ears. And then she looks down.

She cannot help herself. She crouches and peers beneath the desk, hoping to find her mother's journal where it fell. It is not there, but halfway to the door she glimpses a bit of paper in the corner, its left edge torn.

On it, her mother's hand, already beginning to slant.

I am afraid it wasn't my hand on her cheek wasn't my voice in my mouth wasn't my eyes watching her sleep

She shivers, letting the paper fall.

As it whispers to the floor, she hears footsteps overhead. The slow, easy stride of a man at home. Olivia holds her breath and listens until they fade.

Run, says her blood.

Stay, say her bones.

Olivia traces her way back down the maze of halls, not to the grand stairs, broad and bathed in silver light, but to the music room.

She circles the ruined piano, its black and white teeth piled in a heap, and goes to the corner. Her fingers trace the seams, just like Matthew showed her, until she finds the little latch. A gentle press, and the panel swings open onto steep, narrow steps. It is pitch black, and she climbs by feel, counts ten steps before reaching the top.

She turns in the dark and feels for the other door. For a second, it holds, unwilling to give. Fear twists through her, the simple, visceral fear of a body enclosed in a narrow stone space, and in her panic, she throws herself against the door too hard. It swings open, spilling her out into the room.

Olivia almost falls but catches herself on the wooden poster of the bed. She bites her tongue and feels the warm taste of copper in her mouth. Blood. She swallows it and steadies herself. She is in Matthew's room, or at least, the room he lives in on the other side. Here, it is abandoned. The bed sits covered in a film of dust. The shutters are open, the window glass splintered, the tapestry that hung on his wall threadbare and leached of color.

She holds her breath and listens, but the footsteps she heard have stopped. She rounds the bed, goes to the door that leads to the upstairs hall, pressing her ear to the wood. Silence. Her hand goes to the knob, and she's about to ease the door open when she feels as much as hears the sound of a body shifting, the sigh of limbs on a mattress.

Her eyes go back to the four-poster bed. It is still empty. She looks to the tapestry on the wall. And then she is there, guiding the heavy curtain aside, staring at the second door. It is ajar, the wood whispering open under her touch.

There in the dark of the other room, there is a bed. And on the bed, a boy lies curled beneath the sheets.

Olivia starts forward, then catches herself, hands on the doorway. It is too easy. Which is to say, it hasn't been easy at all, but this, this part, feels like a trap. Here is the way in, and there is the bait, and she knows better than to reach for it. Instead she takes a step back.

The trouble is that when she does, the floorboards creak under her feet, and the figure in the bed stirs and sits up. Unfolds, and as it does, she realizes it is not the boy she saw in the fountain, but a shadow. A soldier. The short wolfish one with the feral grin. The gauntlet gleams on her hand as she pulls away the sheet.

Olivia lurches back into Matthew's room, only to collide with another body, one that made no noise when it came in. Out of the corner of her eye, she catches the edge of a tattered black coat.

"Hello, little mouse."

That voice, like smoke in a narrow space. She can hear him smile, teeth clicking together in his open jaw. Her hand slides into the pocket of her dress and closes over Edgar's knife.

"I've been waiting for you."

Olivia spins, drawing the blade. She doesn't wait, but twists and drives the knife into his chest. The master of the house looks down at the weapon protruding from his front and clucks his tongue.

"Now, now," he says, "is that how we treat family?"

He curls his hand around her wrist, his touch like paper over stone. His fingers tighten, and pain lances through her bones, along with something else, the spark of heat, the sudden cold, the same strange dip and fall she felt when she brought the mouse and the flowers back to life. As if he's stealing something from her. Sure enough, the faintest hint of color spreads across his skin, and a wave of dizziness crashes into her, making the room tip and her vision blur. She tears free, surging toward Matthew's bedroom door, toward the hall beyond, only to find another soldier blocking her way. The one built like a brick, armor strapped to his shoulder.

He looks down at her, bored.

Behind her, the master sighs.

"Olivia, Olivia, Olivia," he chides, and the sound of her name in his mouth sends a shiver through her. She scrambles back, turns toward the hidden door only to see the third soldier leaning against the wooden post of the bed, armored plate shining on their chest.

She is surrounded. Trapped.

But not alone.

Help, she thinks, and the man who is not a man must be able to hear her thoughts, because his mouth twitches, amused. But she is not speaking to him.

HELP ME! she calls again, the force of the words shuddering through her.

And they come.

Five ghouls rise up through the rotting floor. Among them, she sees the one who helped her escape. It glances at her now, a sadness sweeping across its half-there face. The ghouls form a circle around Olivia. They have no weapons, but they stand, backs straight, facing out. And for a moment, she feels safe. Protected.

Until the monster *laughs*.

"What a quaint little trick," he says, taking a step toward her. "But I am the master of this house." Another step. "And here, the dead belong to me."

He sweeps his hand through the air, as if brushing away smoke, and the five ghouls twitch and waver. They dissolve, crumbling back into the floor, and she is alone again.

The three soldiers close around her.

Olivia fights.

She fights the way she did back at Merilance, when Anabelle's friends held her down, fights with every ounce of strength and every dirty trick she knows, fights like a girl set loose on the world with nothing and everything to lose. But it's not enough. A gauntlet closes over her wrist, flinging her into an plated chest, and the last thing she sees is the gleam of an armored shoulder as the third shadow looms.

"Mind the hands," says the master, right before pain explodes on the side of her head, and the strength goes out of her limbs, and the world gives way to black.

Chapter Twenty-Six

It died.

The cat Olivia saw that summer on the tin roof, the grouchy old stray that reminded her of Matron Agatha. One day she escaped across the gravel moat to the garden shed and found the animal slumped on the ground nearby.

It was so rangy, so thin.

Olivia could feel its bones beneath its fur as she crouched over the body, ran her hand down its soft side, petting the creature as if it were simply asleep. As if she might be able to bring it back.

Wake up, she thought, tears sliding down her cheeks, even though she hadn't liked the stupid cat.

She buried it in the garden shed, hoping it might haunt her. Hoping that one day she'd catch sight of it out of the corner of her eye, another body in the dark.

She forgot. Isn't that strange? She forgot.

The world comes back in pieces.

The brittle crack of pages turning. The silver light against the crumbling walls. The moldy fabric against her cheek.

She is lying on a sofa. It takes her a moment to realize it is the one in the sitting room, where Hannah brought her that first night at Gallant. Where she sat, tired and confused, as Edgar and Hannah argued about what to do with her, and Matthew came charging in and tore the letter from Hannah's hand and cast it into the fire.

There is no fire now, just a splintered stone hearth. A velvet chair. A low table with an object perched atop it: a helmet. The same polished metal as the pauldron and the chest plate and the gauntlet. She frowns at it, her thoughts too slow.

Her hands are bound together with a length of dark gray rope. She pushes herself up, even though the movement makes her head ache and her vision swim. When it steadies, she sees that she is not alone.

The soldiers stand around the darkened room.

The broad one waits by the door.

The thin one leans against the wall.

The short one rests her elbows on the back of the sofa.

And the master of the house sits in the velvet chair, a blueblack rose balanced on the arm and a book open in his lap.

"Olivia, Olivia, Olivia," he says, and a shiver rolls over her skin as she glimpses the *G* curling across the front of the book.

"I have been whispering the name into your hair," he goes on, and then she is on her feet, lunging toward him, toward her mother's journal, only to feel a large arm catch her around the waist.

The broad soldier hauls her back, and a second later she lands on the sofa again. The short one brings her hands down on Olivia's shoulders, gauntlet rattling as she holds her in place.

"They say there is love in letting go," the master continues, his voice rolling through the room, "but I feel only loss." He flicks ahead as if bored, skipping to the final page.

"Remember this," he says. "The shadows are not real."

His milky eyes float up.

"The dreams can never hurt you."

His mouth curls into a smile.

"And you will be safe as long as you stay away from Gallant."

He closes the journal.

"What would your mother think if she were here?"

He tosses the book onto the low table, where it lands beside the helmet, sending up a plume of dust. "Good thing she's not."

He takes up the rose, and it's one of the blooms she brought back, its head massive, its petals velvet.

"Leave," he says, and for a moment, Olivia thinks he's talking to her, that he's giving her permission to go. But then she realizes the order was given to his soldiers. The broad one retreats. The short one follows. The thin one hesitates, only a moment, before vanishing into the hall.

The door closes.

And they are alone.

She flexes her fingers. Edgar's knife is gone, but she studies the broken stone hearth, searching the fragments on the floor. Would any be light and sharp enough to wield?

The voice drags her attention back.

"Quite a talent you have," he says, studying the wild rose. "And quite a pair we'll make." He lifts the flower to his nose, inhales, and as he does, it wilts again. The petals wither, the head droops, the leaves curl like dry paper. As it dies, the faintest color floods back into his cheeks. Brief as a fish darting underwater.

The rose crumbles to ash, but the ash doesn't fall. Instead it swirls in the air around his hand.

"It is one thing to give death form," he says, and the ashes coalesce into a chalice. "Another to breathe life back into it."

A twitch of his fingers, and the chalice dissolves.

He draws something from his pocket. It is curved and white, save for the point, which is black, as if dipped in ink. A sliver of bone. He holds it out to her, and as he does, the ropes crumble from her wrists.

"Show me," he says, and Olivia stiffens. She should refuse, just to spite him, but an urge takes shape inside her. A longing. Her fingers hum with it. And something else forms there. A question. An idea.

He sets the bone in her hand, and the prickle of life rises through her. It hovers just beneath her skin, waiting to be unleashed.

Live, she thinks, and the feeling rushes forward, out of her hand and into the remains, and as it does, the sliver of bone becomes a beak, becomes a skull, becomes a crow, muscle and skin and feathers. In seconds it is whole again, yawning wide as if to caw, but the only sound she hears is the master's soft chuckle.

The crow clicks its beak, one black eye finding hers, and for a moment, she marvels at the feat of it, the power in her hands. And then—

Attack, she thinks, and the crow bursts into the air and dives for the creature in the chair, and Olivia is on her feet, racing toward the door, even as she hears him pluck the bird from the air, the brittle snap of its neck, even when he says, *"My dearest niece, I confess, I do not know exactly where you are."*

Her steps slow. Her uncle's letter.

"You were not easy to find. Your mother hid you well."

Go, she thinks, even as she finds herself turning back to face him.

"We must thank Hannah," he says, and Olivia flinches at the sound of the woman's name, wishes she could steal it back. "She made the list of all the places you might be."

The notebook in the study drawer. But Olivia checked the desk in *this* study. There was no journal there.

"The two houses are bound. The walls are thin. And I have a way of reaching Prior minds when they are inside Gallant."

Olivia's heart sinks. Matthew.

"A body needs sleep. Without it, the heart gets weak. The

mind gets tired. And tired minds are pliable things."

As he speaks, the images float behind her eyes like waking dreams. Matthew, rising from his bed. Moving slowly through the house, his eyes half-open, no longer blue-gray but milky white.

"Speak to the tired and they listen."

I don't remember falling asleep, her mother wrote.

"Whisper to them and they move."

But I woke up and I was standing over Olivia.

"A tired body doesn't care. It's like a seed, designed to carry."

She sees Matthew moving down the darkened hall into the study, sees him draw the little black book from the top drawer, even though he cannot read, those borrowed eyes tracking over the list of homes that were not homes.

"I have sent these letters to every corner of the country," recites the master of the house. *"May this be the one that finds you. You are wanted. You are needed. You belong with us."*

Behind her eyes, Matthew's face collapses in anger. He casts the letter into the fire. *"I don't know who sent you that letter. But it was not my father."*

The master rises from his chair.

"Come home, dear niece. We cannot wait to welcome you."

He smiles, that eerie, rictus grin. But Olivia shakes her head. He said that Prior minds were his, so long as they were bound to Gallant. But her mother left. And still he followed her.

"Grace was different," he says. "It didn't matter how far she went. So long as she carried a piece of *me* with her."

He turns his head, and she sees the rent in his cheek where the skin pulls back, exposing jaw and teeth. And that is when she sees the hole. The dark hollow in the back of his mouth.

When you came apart, I found the cursed bone. It was a molar, of all things, his mouth hiding inside yours.

She sees him standing in the ballroom, his skin, tattered with so many missing bones. The ash-born dancers, how they collapsed to dust, and how he called the slivers back, the borrowed fragments of himself. How the skin only healed when the bones returned home.

I ground the tooth to dust, her mother wrote. *And threw the filings on the fire. He will never have the piece that was you. I hope he rots while worrying the hole.*

The tooth is gone. The piece of him. Her mother made sure of that. How did he find her then? How—oh. Oh no.

At least I have Olivia.

She is the reason her mother could not escape the dreams. The reason he could get into her head, no matter how far they fled. Because half of her is his.

"And here you are. Where you belong."

She backs away from the words, from him.

There is no one between her and the door and she throws herself against it, expecting him to lunge for her before she makes it, expecting to find it locked. But it gives, swinging open, and she plunges out into the darkened hall.

She rounds the corner only to find the narrow soldier waiting at the end. She staggers backward, turns down another hall, try-ing to orient herself in the dark.

She sprints through the maze of crumbling walls.

Too loud, too loud, she thinks, every step, every breath, every cracking board beneath her feet. Her bones tell her to hide. Her heart tells her to run. Every inch of her screams to get out, get away, get back to the wall, but she has to find Thomas. She scans the open doors, the rooms beyond.

Where are you? Where are you? Where are you? she pleads, skidding around the corner.

That horrible voice echoes through the silent house.

"Olivia, Olivia, Olivia."

She catches her toe on a threadbare rug and goes down hard, pain shooting through her hands as she throws them out to break her fall.

Metal glints as the broad soldier rounds the corner. She scrambles to her feet.

"This is your home."

Where is the nearest hidden tunnel?

"This is the only house that will ever welcome you."

Where is Thomas Prior?

"Once you understand, you will not want to leave."

She bursts through a set of doors and into the ballroom, sprawling and dark. She is halfway to the far wall and the wooden molding and the hidden door when she hears the skitter like pebbles thrown across the inlaid floor.

And the room surges to life.

One moment it is empty, and the next, the dancers rise up to every side, from ashes to flesh in a single breath. They twirl around her, skirts whispering and shoes hissing, a turning wall of bodies. They open their mouths and the voice that pours out is his, only his.

"You cannot run from me."

The dancers part to let him through. Beneath his tattered coat, his skin is broken in a dozen places, one for every missing piece. The three soldiers follow in his wake, and the dancers close behind them and fall still.

"I know what they have told you. That this is a prison, and I am the prisoner. But they are wrong. I am not a monster to be caged."

He catches Olivia's bandaged hand.

"I am simply nature. I am the cycle. The balance. And I am inevitable. The way night is inevitable. The way death is inevitable."

He runs a bony finger down the line of the cut across her palm.

"And you, my darling, are going to let me out."

Olivia twists free, turns away, but there is nowhere to go. The dancers stand still as cell bars, the soldiers spaced between them.

"Do you want to hear a story?"

She turns back toward the voice as he tosses two bones onto the ballroom floor.

Olivia watches as the bits of bone twitch on the patterned wood and begin to grow. Each a seed, the ash twining up like weeds until it forms limbs, bodies, faces.

Until they are right there in the ballroom.

Her parents.

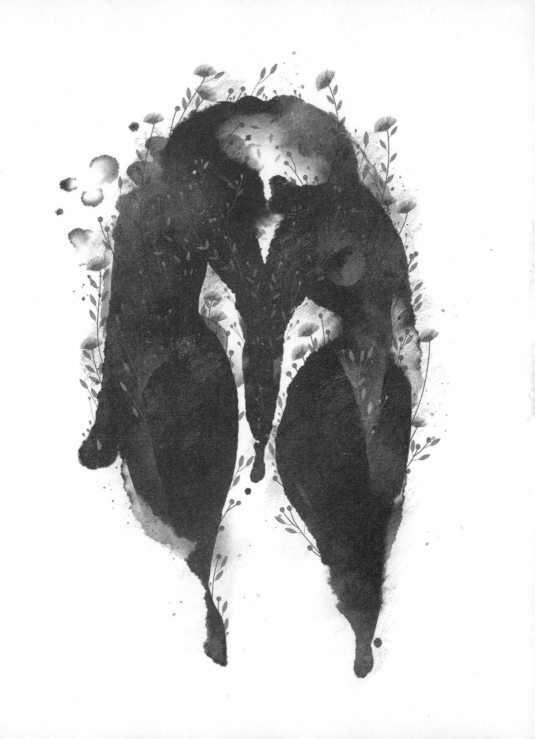

Chapter Twenty-Seven

Even though their clothes are faded and their skin is pale, even though Olivia has just seen them conjured out of bone and dust, even though she knows that they are not really there, that they are dead, they look so solid.

So real.

Olivia stares up into another version of her mother's face, not the girl in the portrait or the ghoul in the bed, but Grace Prior as she must have been when she first stole beyond the wall, in a summer dress that skims her knees, her hair braided up into a crown.

Look at me, thinks Olivia, willing her mother to meet her gaze, but she has eyes only for the other conjured shape. Her father. He stands several feet away, a helmet in his hands. He stares down into its metal face. And then his gaze drifts up and Olivia sees her own eyes staring back, her own charcoal hair curling across his brow, the pieces of herself she could never place.

"He was the first of my four shadows," says the master of the house. "I made him. I made them all, of course, but he was my first. My favorite."

Her father lifts the helmet and puts it on, the metal curving against his cheeks. And the master stares at him, anger etched across his face.

"The longer a shadow lives, the more it becomes . . . itself. The more it thinks for itself. Feels for itself." He glances at the other three soldiers. "A lesson I've since learned." His white eyes drag back toward her father. "He was stubborn, headstrong and proud. But he was still mine. And she took him."

As he speaks, her parents begin to move like puppets in a play, drifting toward each other across the ballroom floor.

Why do you stay in that place?

Her mother lifts the helmet from his face. He takes it from her, sets it down. She pulls him close.

If I gave you my hand, would you take it?

Her father bows his head toward hers. She whispers in his ear.

Free—a small word for such a magnificent thing.

He glances back at the master as her hand finds his. As she draws him in her wake.

I don't know what it feels like, but I want to find out.

Don't you?

And there is no garden wall, no conjured set, but Olivia knows what happens next.

We made it. We are free. And yet—

"And yet, puppets cannot live without their strings. I could have told her that."

Olivia does not want to see what happens next. But she cannot look away.

Something is wrong, her mother wrote. And it is. In the room, her father stumbles, unsteady on his feet.

I can see you withering. I am afraid tomorrow I will see straight through you. I am afraid the next, you will be gone.

"I tried to tell her," says the master of the house. "I whispered in her head. I shouted through her dreams. I told her she must bring him back to me. Or . . ."

Her father staggers, collapses to his hands and knees. His skin so thin over his bones, his body withering before her eyes.

Olivia rushes forward, but the master catches her wrist. "Watch."

Her father looks up then, and for a moment, just a moment, his eyes meet hers, and he sees her, he *sees* her, she swears that he sees her. His mouth opens and closes, forming her name.

"Olivia," he says, and it is the master's voice, not his, but the sound of it still cracks her open, wraps cold hands around her heart.

And then, as she watches, as her mother watches, as they all watch, her father crumbles, a plume of ash by the time his body hits the floor.

"She should have brought him back to me."

It wasn't her father. She tells herself it wasn't her father, just a mimic, an echo, but her hands are still shaking. The bit of bone sits in the puddle of ash.

"Perhaps I lost my temper then."

Her mother stares in horror at the empty space. She sinks to her knees on the ballroom floor.

"I did not make you, but I made the thing that did, and I could feel you out there, like a piece of me. A missing bone. You are mine, and she refused to bring you home."

Her mother presses her palms against her ears as if something is screaming inside her head.

Stop, thinks Olivia, as her mother folds forward, running her hands through her hair, the braided crown now loose, her body thin and brittle.

Stop.

"If she had only listened."

STOP.

Her mother collapses back into dust, leaving only a sliver of bone on the ballroom floor. Olivia stares down at the ashes, hands clenching into fists. Tears burn her eyes, angry and hot.

And then, the master of the house does something worse.

He brings them back.

A flick of his thin fingers, and the ashes bloom around the bones again, until her parents are on their feet, exactly as they were before, her father reaching down to take up the helmet, her mother watching him with wonder. All the fear and horror has been wiped from their faces. They look to each other, as if for the first time, and the horrible play begins again.

Olivia tries to back away, only to feel armor plate against her shoulders. The wisp-thin soldier blocking her way.

"Do you know what you are, Olivia Prior? You are amends. You are atonement for your father's defiance and your mother's theft. You are a tithe, a gift, and you belong to me."

Her parents drift together on the ballroom floor. Their hands entwine. Her mother leans in to whisper in her father's ear. Olivia cannot stand to watch it all again.

Why are you doing this? she thinks, tearing her gaze away.

"This?" He sweeps a hand at the ash-born players, and they stop, mid-stride. "This is what I'm offering."

Olivia shakes her head. She doesn't understand.

"You are not just a Prior," he says, stepping toward her. "Here, you are something more." He looks down at her with those white eyes. "I can shape death," he says, gesturing to the conjured figures. "But you can give it life."

Understanding washes over her like cold water.

Her parents turn to look at her. Waiting.

"You belong here with your family. And for a drop of blood on an old iron door, you can have them back."

Her father embraces her mother.

Her mother reaches for Olivia.

"In your hands, the house will mend. The gardens will grow. You will be happy. You will be home."

It would be a lie to say she doesn't want it.

A lie to say she isn't tempted.

A drop of blood for this. For a family. For a home.

Wouldn't it be worth it?

You belong here.

She looks down at herself, the way she blends into the grays of this world. This world, where no one but the master speaks, yet everyone can hear her. This world, where she would never be alone again.

Her mother smiles, and she can imagine the color flooding back into her cheeks. Her father looks at her with love, with pride.

Her palms begin to burn.

But they are not her parents.

Her mother was flesh and blood and human, and she is a ghoul in her family's house. Her father may have started out like this, born of ash and shadow, but he became more. And even though she never met him, she knows he would not have wanted this.

This is a dream.

It would be so easy to climb inside, to stay until it felt real, to never wake up.

But somewhere in this house, Thomas is waiting.

Back at the wall, Matthew is waiting.

Inside Gallant, Hannah and Edgar are waiting.

And even if Olivia could live in this cold gray world, she doesn't want to. She wants the vivid colors of the garden at Gallant and the sound of the piano spilling through the halls, Hannah's kind hands and the way Edgar hums whenever he's cooking.

She wants to go home.

Olivia turns to the soldier at her back. She reaches up, touches her fingers against their face, takes all the heat gathering beneath her skin, and pushes it into the shadow.

"NO!" snarls the master of the house, and a second later ash spins around her fingers, forming itself into a pair of silken gloves.

But it is too late. The soldier staggers back a single step, and then looks up, light flooding in their cheeks, and fire in their eyes. Alive.

Olivia shivers, overcome by a sudden, awful chill, the cost of her own magic. But there is no time.

Fight for me, she thinks through chattering teeth, and the soldier draws their blade, and charges past her. The room plunges into chaos, then, as the dancers jostle, and the other two soldiers draw their weapons, and the master stands at the center of the storm. In the chaos, Olivia breaks out of the circle and runs across the ballroom to the wooden molding, gloved hands groping for the hidden door.

She is still shaking violently as she finds the latch, and the tiny door swings in, and she looks back only to see the master's long sharp fingers tear the soldier's armor off and plunge into their chest, and for a terrible moment she thinks she will see the master drawing out a heart. His blood-stained hand comes free, but there is no beating heart, only a single rib. Still, the soldier shudders and collapses, and the master spins round, looking for Olivia, but she is already dropping through the hidden door into the dark.

She crouches, knees scraping the stone stairs. It is too low to stand.

Her whole body shivers as she claws at the gloves, but she can't get them off. They wrap around her hands like a second skin. The chill finally begins to ebb, leaving her breathless on the steps.

Down in the cellar, something moves. A whisper of motion— the quiet rasp of a body sliding over dirt. She twists, almost losing her balance as she looks past the six steps into the cellar below.

Her shoes slide on the damp, slick stone as she climbs down. There are no windows, no open doors, no cracks for the light to slip in, if there were any light outside—and yet, when she reaches the packed dirt floor, she can *almost* see. The silver glow that seems to come from the house itself seeps like damp from the wood and the stone. She blinks, eyes adjusting.

The floor is littered with broken jars and empty crates.

A small shape twitches in the dark. A ghoul hiding in the corner between boxes.

Show yourself, she thinks, but the ghoul doesn't drift forward, and as she takes a cautious step, she sees it is not a ghoul at all, but a boy, head bowed, and arms wrapped around his narrow knees.

Thomas.

The master of the house has had enough.

He crouches over the body of his second shadow, the red of their blood staining the floor as he fits the rib back into his own chest, paper skin closing over the bone.

His tongue drifts, as it always does, to the hole in the back of his mouth. The one piece he will never get back.

He presses his hand to the shadow's body, and it withers, life flooding like a current beneath his skin as the corpse turns to dust on the ballroom floor.

The blood dries, too, crumbles, blown away by a stale breeze.

It is only a taste of what he will do.

Hunger gnaws inside him, unyielding, insatiable.

"There is a mouse in my house," he says to the remaining soldiers and the dancers and the ghouls. "Find it."

Part Six
HOME

Chapter Twenty-Eight

Thomas Prior stares up at her, his blue eyes gray in the silver light.

He looks tired and hungry, but he can sleep and eat when they are back beyond the wall. All that matters now is that he is alive, and Olivia has found him. She wants to throw her arms around his narrow shoulders, but he looks as if the force might break him, so instead she kneels, her face inches from his, hoping that he can see the echoes in her brow, her eyes, her cheeks, and know that they are family.

Thomas frowns and opens his mouth as if to speak, but she clamps a gloved hand over his lips as the voice rings out through the house overhead.

"Olivia, Olivia, Olivia!" it calls. *"Do you really think you can hide in my house?"*

Thomas shivers at the sound of the master's voice, and she draws her hand from his mouth, holding just a finger to his lips. She scans the cellar. There are two sets of stairs, the one down from the ballroom and the one up to the kitchen, and she is about to guide Thomas to the second set when he rises on unsteady legs and begins to drag a crate across the cellar floor.

It makes a horrible sound, like nails on stone, and she lunges forward, pinning him still, holding her breath and hoping the thing overhead didn't hear. And then her eyes go to the crate, not where it is now, in the middle of the room, but where it was before, in front of the shelves. Beyond the metal racks and behind the empty jars is a piece of wood, the size of a very small door.

My brother made a game of it, finding all the secret places.

Olivia kneels in front of the shelf and shifts the jars, one by one, careful not to rattle them. And then she crouches low and slides the wooden panel out of the way. She peers through, hoping to see night, to see the dead grass and winding thorns of the garden.

But all she sees is black.

She turns and finds Thomas staring up at the ceiling, eyes wide with fear as the master of the house rants and rages overhead.

Olivia holds out her hand, and his gaze drops to meet hers.

It's okay, she thinks, even though he cannot hear her. *We are almost there,* she thinks, *and your brother is waiting.*

His hand slides into hers, thin fingers clutching at the strange silk gloves, and she draws him forward into the dark. They crawl on hands and knees through the pitch-black tunnel, and she tries not think of a grave, of a tomb, of being buried here, under the house that is not Gallant.

And then, finally, she feels the panel on the other side. It slides out of the way, and there, at last, is the garden, the sky, the cool night air. Even though it tastes like moldy leaves and soot instead of grass and summer, she gulps it in, grateful to be out of the house.

She pulls Thomas to his feet, and together they run through the garden toward the waiting wall.

She doesn't look back to see if the soldiers are coming.

Doesn't look back to see if the master is watching from the balcony.

Thorns catch on her dress and she doesn't look back.

Ivy scrapes her legs, and she doesn't look back.

They reach the iron gate in the center of the wall, and Olivia's gloved hand slides free of Thomas's as she flings herself against the door, pounding on it, the iron itself buried beneath layers of debris. The sound is swallowed up before it reaches air, but Matthew must have been waiting, must have had his cheek against the metal, because a moment later she hears the hum of a lock turning deep inside the iron, and then it swings open, and he is there, Gallant rising at his back.

His eyes go wide as they slide from her to Thomas. He grips the gate, clearly resisting the urge to run forward, to wrap his arms around his brother. Olivia holds out a gloved hand for the boy, but when he steps forward, a shadow crosses Matthew's face.

"Wait," he says, studying Thomas.

Olivia looks back. The garden is no longer empty. She can see the glint of armor at the top of the garden, the milk-white eyes like candles in the dark. Her hand cuts through the air.

Get out of the way, she orders, grabbing Thomas's hand and barging forward, but Matthew bars the door.

"Say something," he demands, and for a moment Olivia thinks he's talking to *her,* but his eyes are still on the boy. Thomas looks up at Matthew and says nothing.

And for the first time, she sees him as Matthew must. His fair hair, made gray by the silver light. His skin, pale from the years without sun. His eyes, not warm, but cool and dark.

A terrible sadness rolls through her as she watches the hope bleed out of her cousin's face.

He shakes his head and says, "That's not my brother."

Olivia looks at Thomas, his hand vising around hers. She can feel his heart beating, can hear his lungs filling. He feels so real. But then, so did the dancers, so did the soldiers, so did her mother and father, and she saw them grown from nothing but a finger bone and a cloud of ash. This is not a boy. This is a gray thing, conjured from death.

But she could breathe life into him.

Beneath the silk gloves, her palms begin to burn. She has power here. This may not be Matthew's brother, but it could be. If she brought him back, if—but she cannot do it. Not to Matthew, or Thomas.

Just like her parents, he wouldn't be real.

He would never be able to step across the wall. He would be trapped here, all over again.

"Olivia," warns Matthew, "get away from him," and she realizes she's not holding on to the boy anymore. The boy is holding on to her. He clutches her hand so hard it hurts, his small fingers digging into her glove as the shadows slide through the garden.

"Let *go*," orders Matthew, gripping the doorway, but she *can't*. The bones grind in her hand, and she gasps, trying to twist free, as the boy pulls her close, wraps his thin arms around her, and seems to grow roots.

And then the boy who is not Thomas smiles. A terrible, sinister grin. This time, when he opens his mouth to speak, a voice comes out.

The only voice beyond the wall.

"Olivia, Olivia, Olivia," it purrs. "What will we do with you?"

His embrace tightens until she cannot move, cannot breathe. Her bones groan, and she lets out a stifled gasp, and then Matthew is surging through the door. He makes it a few feet before turning back and pulling the gate closed behind him, the warm summer night and safety and home vanishing behind the wall. He presses a bloody hand to the door and says the words, sealing them in. And then he is there, trying to pry the puppet's arms from Olivia.

"Hold on," he says. "Hold on, I've got you."

The boy's eyes flick to Matthew. "I called your brother and he came."

He shakes his head, trying not to listen to the voice.

"I cut his little throat."

"*Stop,*" snarls Matthew, drawing a dagger, fingers shaking as he moves to hack at the puppet posing as his brother. But before the blade can pierce skin, the skin simply crumbles. The ash-born boy collapses back into dust, a shard of bone abandoned in the withered grass.

Olivia stumbles, suddenly free. She gasps for air and straightens, only to see the two remaining soldiers closing in. The broad one frowns. The short one smirks.

And behind them comes the master of the house.

He makes his way down the garden path, tattered black coat billowing in the stale air. His black hair rises, wild, and his white eyes shine, and when he smiles, the skin of his cheek cracks and splinters like old stone.

Olivia feels Matthew's fingers closing over hers. A single squeeze, and he does not need to speak for her to understand.

Run.

He drops her hand, and she surges toward the wall, looks back to find him standing his ground, a frail young man with nothing but a dagger. She hesitates, unsure if she can really leave him.

But in the end, it doesn't matter.

Olivia is halfway to the wall when the broad shadow steps into her path, armor srapped across his shoulder.

Her fingers twitch, and she wishes she had Edgar's knife or a stick or a stone or anything sharp, though she's not sure what good it would do against the soldier. She tries to dart out of his grip, to make it to the wall. He is large, but she is quick, under his arm and almost to the door before his hands close around her. Before the force of his grip nearly lifts her off her feet.

Help! thinks Olivia, calling on the ghouls, and they come, out of the withered orchard and up through the ruined garden. But at the sight of the grim figure in the tattered coat they stop and shrink away, dissolving again into the night.

Come back! she calls out, but this time, they do not answer. It is her will against his.

And here, the dead belong to me.

And so she fights against the soldier, bucks and kicks, desperate to get free.

"So much life for a thing half-dead," says the master of the house, amused. "And speaking of half-dead . . ."

He turns to Matthew. Her cousin slashes out with his blade, but the wolfish soldier dodges lithely and kicks him in the chest. He collapses to his hands and knees, gasping for breath, and she draws her sword, gauntleted fingers flexing around the hilt.

"Two Priors in my garden," purrs the demon in the dark. "And they said that it was barren."

Matthew tries to get to his feet, but the soldier kicks out his knees. The master of the house strides forward.

"Your brother died for nothing, Matthew Prior. And so will you."

The soldier lowers the dagger to his throat. Olivia lets out a panicked breath. But when Matthew meets her gaze, he doesn't look afraid. He has been waiting for this. Waiting to lie down.

To rest. He has not been afraid to die, not since his brother and father did. He is ready. He is willing.

But there is a question in his eyes. *Are you?*

Olivia Prior does not want to die.

She has only just begun to live.

But they are the only thing standing between the monster and the wall, between death and the living world. And so she nods, and he closes his eyes and swallows against the soldier's blade, relieved. And when he speaks, there is no quaver in his voice.

"It does not matter," he says. "You cannot take our blood by force, and we will not give it to you."

The master does not seem surprised.

"Your honor is charming," he says, approaching the wall. "And wasted. You say you refuse to open the door for me." He smiles, fingers dancing over the stones. "But you already have. Or rather, you failed to close it."

Matthew's head jerks toward the gate, the sheen of his blood visible even in the low silver light. Olivia saw him seal the door. She heard him say the words.

Those long fingers lift to the old iron gate. The master's hand hovers over the door.

"The thing about old houses is the upkeep. How quickly they fall into disrepair." He speaks as if to the gate itself. "Everything decays. Iron rusts. Bodies rot. Leaves dry and break. And all of it turns to dust and ash. No wonder it's hard to keep any surface clean."

He brings a single bony finger to the surface of the door.

"Blood on iron," he says. "Not blood on earth. Not blood on stone. Not blood on ivy. Blood on *iron*. That is the key."

The master drags his nail down the bloody mark on the door, and the surface flakes away, debris crumbling to reveal the iron beneath, untouched.

"No," whispers Matthew, the last color leaching from his face.

"And now," says the monster, "for my final trick."

He presses his hand to the door and gives it a gentle push.

It swings open.

Open onto a summer night. Onto a sprawling garden, a riot of blooms and leaves.

Onto Gallant.

"NO!" roars Matthew, lurching against the soldier's blade, which cuts a shallow line along his throat. The soldier clucks her tongue, and Olivia watches, horrified, as the master of the house steps through the garden door. Even in the dark, she can see the shadows spill around him, can see them sprawl across the grass, can see them eating through land and life.

The master's head falls back, chin tipping up to a sky with a moon and stars. He inhales deeply, as all around him the grass withers and dies, and as it does, his hair curls like night against his cheeks, and his skin looks less like paper than marble, and his tattered cloak turns to velvet, rich and smooth over his shoulders.

He is no longer wasted, but beautiful, horrible.

He is not a monster, not the master of the house, not a demon trapped behind a wall. In that moment, he is Death.

He glances back through the door, eyes as bright as moons, and looks at Olivia with something like fondness before he smiles and says, in a voice as rich as midnight:

"Kill them both."

Chapter Twenty-Nine

The soldiers smile.

The broad one tightens his arms around Olivia's chest, crushing the air from her lungs, and the short one threads her hand through Matthew's hair and wrenches his head back as Death vanishes beyond the wall.

She writhes and tries to breathe, tries to think as time slows down, the world slows down, reduced to light and shadow, to the blade on Matthew's skin and the moonlight beyond the wall. She slams her head back into the soldier, hoping to hit his head, but he is too big, she is too small, and instead, her skull bangs against his armored shoulder.

Pain bursts behind her eyes. Pain, followed by a thought.

The armor.

It seemed so random, the way it was shared between the soldiers. A helmet here, a chest plate there, a gauntlet, a pauldron. But it's not random at all.

Everything the master conjures, he forms around a bone.

Her father had his molar. The wisp-thin soldier had a rib.

The armor shields the borrowed pieces.

And without them—

Olivia writhes with all her strength, kicks her legs back into the soldier's body, forcing just enough distance between them that she can free a hand, reach for the blade at the soldier's hip.

She draws the weapon, drives it blindly back into the soldier's side, and though it doesn't seem to *hurt* him, it is enough of a surprise that he loosens his grip.

Olivia scrambles free, taking the blade with her, but doesn't run.

Instead she turns back and brings the sword down on the armor, metal on metal ringing like a bell.

The short soldier looks up, the blade still kissing Matthew's neck, but the broad one only flashes a bored smile at Olivia. Until she strikes again, this time hitting the leather that binds the metal to his shoulder. It breaks. The pauldron slips and falls away, and so does the soldier's smirk as there, in the silver light, she sees the white curve of a collarbone.

The soldier rears back, but Olivia is already swinging, bringing the sword down a third time, carving deep into his shoulder. The collarbone comes free. Fury crosses his face, brief as a passing shadow, but he is already falling, body collapsing back into dust as the bone hits the grass.

She rounds to find the last soldier staring, wide-eyed, a feral anger etched across her face as she lifts her sword and drives it down toward Matthew's chest. But she wasn't the only one watching. Matthew catches her sword hand, gripping the gauntlet with the last of his strength. He tries to rip the armor off, but the soldier tears free and dances back out of reach, a shadow blending into the dark, and then Olivia is there, pulling her cousin up, away from the shadow and toward the open door. Ten steps, five, one, and then they're through.

Through, into warmth, into soft earth and the smell of rain and the airy night.

Through, into Gallant.

She stumbles to her hands and knees, the gloves crumbling from her fingers, leaving only a streak of ash on barren ground, the magic lost beyond the wall. But the master of the house looks more alive than ever. He makes his way up the garden, fingers trailing over flowers, and rot spreads along the petals and the stems, consuming everything like fire, leaving a ruined black tide in his wake.

In the moments since he stepped through the door, ivy has spilled out, woody vines that force the gate open like a mouth. There is no way to lock the door, not without closing it first. Two spades lie on the ground nearby and Matthew presses one into her hands.

"Start breaking it free," he says as he hefts the other spade and surges up the slope toward Death.

Olivia hacks at ivy, and when that doesn't work, she pulls at it with her bare hands, feels the thorny bark tear open the skin on her palms. Steals a look back over her shoulder, up the slope to the garden as Matthew reaches the grim shadow and swings the spade at his back. But the tool never touches him. It grazes the air around his cloak, and the iron rusts, and the wood rots, and all of its crumbles.

Matthew stumbles back as the monster turns, his eyes a glowing white.

"You are nothing," he says, in a voice like frost.

"I am a Prior," answers Matthew, standing his ground. He has no weapon, nothing in his hands but blood. It stains his palm as he lifts one hand, like the statue in the fountain. "We bound you once, and we will bind you again."

A laugh like thunder rolls through the night.

Olivia keeps hacking at the ivy, even though it's not working, and the door is jammed open, and even if Matthew finds a way to force the monster back, her heart pounds in her chest, warning that there is *no hope, no hope*, no running from death, no hiding from death, no conquering death. But she doesn't stop. She will not stop.

"Olivia!" shouts Matthew, voice ringing in the dark, and she is trying, she is trying. The ivy finally begins to snap and give.

"Olivia!" he calls again, boots pounding over ground as a massive wooden tendril breaks and the door groans free and she looks up in time to see the wolfish soldier inches from her face, in time to see her blade singing through the air.

She doesn't close her eyes.

She is proud of that. She doesn't close her eyes as the sword comes down. It strikes her hard, and she falls, hitting the ground. Waits for pain she doesn't feel. Wonders why she isn't dead, until she looks up at the open door and sees Matthew.

Matthew, standing in her place. Matthew, who pushed her out of the way the instant before the sword cut down.

Matthew, who leans in the doorway, the blade driven through, the point jutting like a thorn from his back.

Olivia screams.

There is no sound to it, but it is there, ringing through her chest, her bones, it is all she can hear as she pushes to her feet and rushes toward the door, toward him.

Too late, she reaches him.

Too late, she brings the spade down on the soldier's gauntlet, severing the armored hand. Too late, the soldier sneers and crumbles, and so does the gauntlet and the sword, and Matthew takes a single, unsteady step back, and falls, Olivia sinking with him.

Her hands race over his front, trying to stem the blood as Matthew coughs and winces.

"Stop him," he pleads, and when she doesn't move, his hand digs hard into her wrist.

"Olivia," he says, "you are a Prior."

The words ripple through her.

Matthew swallows and says again, "Stop him."

Olivia nods. She forces herself to rise and turn to the garden and storm up the path, ready to face Death.

Chapter Thirty

When Olivia was eight, she decided she would live forever.

It was a strange whim, sprouting up like a weed one day between her thoughts. Perhaps it was after the cat by the shed, or when she realized that her father was gone, that her mother was never coming back. Perhaps it was when one of the younger girls took ill, or when the head matron made them sit on the stiff wooden pews and learn of martyrs. She doesn't exactly remember when she had the thought. Only that she had it. That at some point, she simply decided that other things might die, but she would not.

It seemed sound enough.

After all, Olivia had always been a stubborn girl.

If death ever came for her, she would fight, as she fought Anabelle, as she fought Agatha, as she fought everyone who got in her way. She would fight, and she would win.

Of course, she wasn't sure how to fight a thing like death. She assumed that when the time came, she would know how.

She does not.

Olivia runs up the path, grass breaking underfoot as she

passes withered blooms and ruined trees, rotting arches and crumbling stone. She reaches the man who is not a man, the master of the other house, the monster who made her father and killed her mother, and throws herself against him.

She presses her hands flat against his coat and tries to summon the power she felt beyond the wall, imagines herself drawing it back, prying the garden from his grip, the life he stole with every step, taking the marble polish from his cheeks and the shine from his hair. She digs her fingers into Death and tries to take it back.

His white eyes drift down to meet hers.

"Foolish little mouse," he says, voice like a tree felled by a storm. "You have no power here."

Cold steals up her hands where they meet his coat, a teeth-rattling tired, a dire need to close her eyes and sleep. She tries to pull free, but her hands only sink deeper, as if he were a cavern, boneless, bottomless, and there is something she has to do, but as the chill seeps through her, she cannot breathe, cannot think, cannot—

A gun goes off, the blast shattering the night.

Hannah and Edgar stand at the top of the garden.

Olivia tears free, staggers back, her vision swimming as Edgar aims at Death a second time and fires, the bullet melting in the air above his floating cloak. They cannot kill him, they know they cannot kill him, but they will die protecting Gallant, because it is their home.

They will die and haunt this place like—

Like ghouls.

Shadows skate up the garden path, thin as fingers, killing every leaf and stem as they reach for Hannah, for Edgar, but Olivia throws herself between Death and Gallant.

Help me, she thinks, the word reaching like roots beneath the soil. *Help me protect our home.*

And they come.

They rise up from the ground. They step out of the orchard and drift down from the house. Hannah and Edgar watch, eyes wide, as the ghouls pour into the ruined garden, edges lit by magic and moonlight.

Olivia watches, too. Watches her mother, hair loose and wild, stride through the roses, her uncle march forward, hands balling into fists, watches the old man and the young woman and a dozen other faces she never knew. They come, armed with shovels and blades.

Death glances down at her, amused. "We've been through this already, little mouse. Weren't you listening?"

And she was.

The ghouls beyond the wall belong to him.

But the ones at Gallant, she thinks, *belong to me.*

The smile drops from his face.

He turns to the ghouls as they gather around him. Old and young. Strong and wasted. How many did he ruin? How many did he kill? Down at the wall, beyond the open door, the other

Priors stand, waiting to drag him home. And there at the front of them, she sees the boy. The one who lived and died two years ago beyond the wall.

The monster cuts his hand through the air, and a few of them ripple, but none of them fade.

"You are nothing," he sneers as they close in. "You cannot kill me."

And he is right, of course. You cannot kill death. That is why you banish it.

They close over him like ivy, their edges dissolving into one teeming mass of shadow as they force him back through the garden, back through the open door, back beyond the wall.

They strike it like a wave crashing onto shore.

Olivia rushes in their wake, her hands slick with blood, some hers and some Matthew's. She reaches the iron gate and slams it shut, presses her palms to the metal and thinks, *With my blood, I seal this door.*

The lock hums inside the iron.

The door seals itself against the wall, the other side swallowed up behind iron and stone. The garden falls silent. The night goes still. Hannah and Edgar rush through the dark, toward her and the shape lying on the sloping ground.

Matthew.

Olivia gets there first, sinking to her knees beside his head. He is so still, eyes gazing up at the sky, and she is afraid he is already gone, but then his lids flutter and his breathing slows, a body on the edge of sleep.

"Is it done?" he says, the words more shape than sound, and Olivia nods as Hannah crouches on the other side. Edgar stands, one hand on Hannah's shoulder.

"Oh, Matthew," she says, gently, stroking his hair.

Perhaps he will be okay. Perhaps he simply needs to rest. Perhaps, but as she kneels beside him, she can feel the blood, soaking into the ground, staining her skin. There is so much of it.

"Olivia," he says softly, fingers twitching. She takes his hand, bows her head close. "Stay," he whispers. "Until I fall asleep."

She grits her teeth against tears and nods.

"I don't . . ." He falters then, swallows. "I don't want to be alone."

He isn't, of course. She is there, and so are Hannah and Edgar. And then, out of the darkness comes the ghoul. Arthur Prior sinks to the ground beside his son. He reaches out a hand and strokes the air beside his head. And finally, Matthew closes his eyes and rests.

He doesn't wake again.

But they stay there with him until dawn.

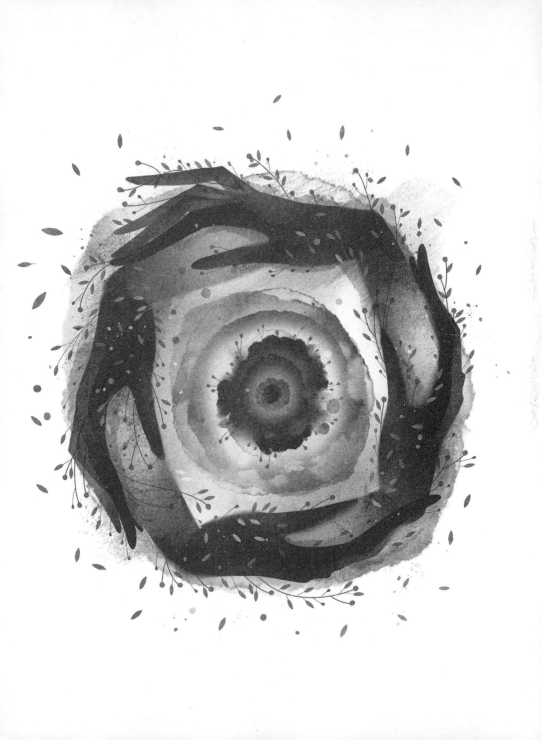

Olivia kneels among the roses.

A cold breeze rolls through the garden, snatching loose leaves and drooping petals and whisking them away, summer finally losing its hold.

She hisses at the autumn chill, pulling her jacket close. It is her mother's, the coat, a bold blue thing trimmed with white. It is still too big on her, but sleeves can be rolled, and hems lifted, and one day, she knows, it will fit. For now, it keeps the breeze at bay, and the thorns from snagging on her skin as she prunes the gray weeds that still fight their way up through the injured ground, twist and tangle through the plants. Persistent, she thinks.

But so is she.

Olivia stands, surveying her work.

Close to the house, a few rose bushes survived, but death has washed like a tide over the rest. It took a week to clear the ruins. To nourish the soil and try to start again.

It will grow back, she tells herself. If death is a part of the cycle, then so is life. All things fade, and all things flourish.

The soil felt good under her hands. Better still when the first thin shoots of new grass began to show.

Edgar says she has a gift for it, a green thumb.

It is not a power, exactly, not like the one she had beyond the wall, but it is something. And in time, with care, the garden at Gallant will come back.

Other things will not.

Her gaze drifts down the slope, stopping before the wall.

There is a smooth white stone set in the middle of the ruined grass. It stands out on the shadowed rise, as bright as bone against the dark gray dirt. Edgar helped her place it, to mark the spot where Matthew fell.

He is not buried there, of course. His body is next to his father's, beyond the orchard in the family plot. But it felt right, and every time she finds her gaze drifting to the door in the wall, it lands here instead.

A reminder, for the nights when the darkness whispers through her head, trying to coax her to come out, come back, come home.

But home is a choice.

And she has chosen Gallant.

There is only one thing she longs for beyond the wall.

A small green book, with a G pressed into the cover.

Her mother's words, her father's drawings.

Her fingers itch, the way they always do when she thinks of the journal.

She pictures the master of the house sitting in his velvet chair, beside the empty hearth, turning the pages and reading aloud to himself.

Olivia, Olivia, Olivia.

She makes her way up through the garden, pail in hand. All the roses are gone now, even those safe against the house, except for one. A single stubborn bush continues to bloom, only a handful of red roses left on the stems.

Olivia cuts one and holds it to her nose out of habit, even though Matthew grew them all for color, not for scent. She will plant some new ones in the spring, ones that can be both.

Up on the balcony, Hannah is pounding out a rug.

She claims there is dust everywhere. A patina of ash that sweeps in through the cracks in the shutters and the gaps beneath the doors and settles over everything. Olivia does not feel it, but every day Hannah scrubs and pounds and clears away the ashes of the night before. Edgar says it is her way of mourning.

The sun slips down the sky as Olivia kicks off her garden boots, leaves them by the back door, and goes inside.

She hears Edgar in the kitchen, making stew. If she listens closely, she can hear him humming. An old hymn he used to sing to patients in the war.

The house is too big for three people, so they each try to take up space, to make noise.

Olivia yawns as she makes her way through the house.

She has not been sleeping well.

Every night, she dreams she is beyond the wall.

Sometimes Death is waiting for her on the balcony, dead eyes burning like stars in the dark.

Sometimes he is calling for her as she runs through the house, desperate to find a way out.

But most times, she is in the ballroom, where he conjures her parents from ash and bone. Over and over she watches them meet. Over and over she watches them crumble. Over and over he brings them back and they look at her with hands out-stretched, with pleading in their eyes, as if to say, we could be real.

They are only dreams, she tells herself, every time she wakes.

And dreams can never hurt you. That's what her mother said. Of course, she knows now it isn't true. Dreams can make you hurt yourself, dreams can make you do so many things, if you're not careful. She has yet to wake and find herself beyond the bed, but she keeps the soft leather cuffs tucked beneath the mattress, in case one day she needs them.

And she is not alone.

Hannah locks the doors each night.

Edgar checks the shutters.

And her mother's ghoul sits at the foot of her bed, eyes trained on the dark.

Olivia moves through the house, thinking of the bath she plans to draw, soaking the dirt of the garden from her limbs. But first, her feet carry her as they always do.

To the music room.

Beyond the bay window, the sun continues to sink. Soon it will fall between the distant mountains and vanish behind the garden wall. But right now, there is still light.

A yellow vase sits on top of the piano, and Olivia sets the red rose there, then sinks onto the narrow bench. She eases up the lid, fingers sliding through the air above before coming to rest on the black and white keys.

The light in the room begins to thin, and out of the corner of her eye, she sees it. The ghoul is half-there, half-not, but she can fill in the missing pieces from memory. The furrowed brow, the messy curls, the eyes, once fever bright. The ghoul draws forward, lowering itself onto the bench beside her. As badly as she wants to turn and look, she doesn't.

She keeps her gaze down and waits, and after a few moments, it bows its half-there head and brings its spectral fingers to the keys. They hover there, waiting for her to follow.

Like this, it seems to say, and she places her hands, just like he showed her, and begins, haltingly, to play.

Acknowledgments

Some stories spill out in a wave. Others come in drips. And now and then, a story sits pooled somewhere, waiting for you to find it. I had to go looking for Olivia's tale. I had the door in the wall, that was always there, but for years, I wasn't certain what I'd find on the other side. What I *needed* to find. Because of that, *Gallant* was not only a work of love, but patience.

In a world with deadlines and release dates and expectations, it is a luxury, to be patient. To have a publishing team that understands that need for patience and makes space for it.

My agent, Holly Root, and my editor, Martha Mihalick, made space, and I will forever be grateful for it. Just as I will be grateful to the entire team at Greenwillow Books, for their confidence and belief when the story I finally found proved strange and wild, and it was clear it wouldn't sit easily on any one shelf, that my readers would still find it.

I am grateful to my cover designer, David Curtis, for creating the perfect door into my world, and to my illustrator, Manuel

Šumberac, for creating pieces of art that have their own voice on the page.

I am grateful to Janice Dubroff for her close reading with respect to nonverbal communication, and to Kristin Dwyer, for being my constant champion, and to Patricia Riley, Dhonielle Clayton, Zoraida Cordova, and Sarah Maria Griffin, for reminding me again and again and again that I know how to do this.

And I am grateful to my mother and father, who were there with me, for once, in person, due to the pandemic. In a time of so many hardships, they provided strength and light, safety and shelter, and the constant reminder that no matter how far I go, how lost I feel, I will always find my way home.